DEPARTING
AT DAWN

More praise for *Departing at Dawn*

"The author offers no apologies or heroes, only humble beings . . . whose portraits are remarkably true-to-life. All kinds of readers will recognize themselves somewhere in this compelling narrative."

—*Artenauta periódico de cultura*

"An intriguing, fast-paced fictional narrative of the 1976 Argentine Dictatorship. This postmodern parable tells the story of a nomadic female subject on her fugitive escape from torture and death."

—Magdalena Maiz-Peña, professor and chair
of Spanish, Davidson College

"As an Argentine who lived through the Years of Lead (1976-82), I remain haunted by survivor's guilt and the need for account-ability. Civil society bears responsibility for state terrorism, so accounts written to prevent a reoccurrence such as Nunca más [*Never Again*] must be complemented by literary renditions. Gloria Lisé's *Departing at Dawn* follows the trail blazed by Alicia Partnoy, Alicia Kozameh, Cristina Feijóo and Nora Strejilevich, and makes a significant contribution to our understanding of that era. Alice Weldon's remarkable translation faithfully renders the tone of this poignant novel."

—Cynthia Margarita Tompkins, associate professor
of Spanish, Arizona State University

"As homage for a generation sacrificed and a call for vigilance against national pogroms, Lisé taps memory as living historical archive to reveal the indomitable Argentine spirit of survival incarnate in its immigrant, indigenous and working class peoples. Highly recommended for high school and college libraries and curricu-lums including English, Latin American, history, women's studies, cultural studies programs."

—Gisela Norat, professor of Spanish, Agnes Scott College

DEPARTING AT DAWN

A Novel of Argentina's Dirty War

Gloria Lisé

TRANSLATED BY ALICE WELDON

THE FEMINIST PRESS
AT THE CITY UNIVERSITY OF NEW YORK
FEMINISTPRESS.ORG

The Feminist Press at the City University of New York
The Graduate Center
365 Fifth Avenue, Suite 5406
New York, NY 10016
Feministpress.org

Originally published in Spanish in 2005.

Library of Congress Cataloging-in-Publication Data

Lisé, Gloria, 1961–
  [Viene clareando. English]
  Departing at dawn / by Gloria Lisé ; translated by Alice Weldon.
      p.   cm.
  ISBN 978-1-55861-603-5 (pbk.) -- ISBN 978-1-55861-604-2 (library cloth)
  I. Title.
  PQ7798.422.I74V5413 2009
  863'7—dc22

                                                    2008034012

13 12 11 10 09   5 4 3 2 1

Contents

ix   Introduction

1   A Pig's Head

4   The Ring

9   A World Within a World

13   This is My Family

19   Listening to the Radio

29   Flowers

35   The Photograph

40   Aunt Avelina

47   Her Body

52   Twenty-one Years Old

57   Tristán Nepomuceno

61   Ave María

68   Perhaps

73   The Messenger

83   Hell

89   The Window

102   Olpa

108   The Indian

114   A Visitor

119   *Cachirú*

124   Lusaper Gregorian

135   Singing

142   *Yacumama*

151   Holy Wood

161   Notes

163   Historical Note

167   Translator's Afterword

To Regina

Thanks to Teresa Leonardi, Antonio Gutiérrez, and
Pancho Galíndez, who still laugh at me; to Mario Benedetti,
bookstore owner in Salta; and to Rossana Caramella.

The story that follows is entirely fiction.

In memory of Isauro Arancibia, his brother,
Atilio Santillán, and Trinidad Iramain, whom I was never
able to meet, because they were killed without ever
being charged or having the right to a defense.

Introduction

ON MARCH 24, 1976, yet another military dictatorship took power in Argentina, and I turned fifteen. It should have been a time in my life for planting the seeds of plans and dreams for the future whose fruit would develop as I matured. My country should have helped make such things possible.

More than ever before my whole body was responding with delight to that southern autumn, as each day seemed to be creating me anew and felt like a fresh beginning. My own strength and beauty, on the threshold of womanhood, held the promise of happiness to come.

Since 1930, however, my country had been living through periods of violence related to numerous changes in government—civil ones followed by ever more violent and longer-lasting military dictatorships.* Even so, the level of repression unleashed by the military arm of the most recent government reached a height never before experienced. I learned about many things the security forces were doing, such as arresting ordinary citizens who were never heard from again. I saw people with scars that evidenced the most despicable torture routinely carried out by soldiers and police in the various places of

* See Historical Note, page 163.

detention. Every day I met children who had lost their mothers, fathers mourning their children, sisters looking for brothers. I saw my country being humiliated and plundered by the very people who called themselves its strongest defenders.

Perhaps the worst part of all this was that, in spite of such dire conditions, most citizens did not denounce what was happening; rather, they defended the military, saying it had taken power only to restore the order and peace that guerrilla groups had disrupted through terrorist acts beginning in the mid-sixties. Besides, many maintained, the last civil government had proven that the citizenry was too politically immature to govern itself, and that the armed forces possessed "the moral force of the nation."

During those years, it was no use looking to the courts for justice against those responsible for the terrorism of the state, because even judges participated in the pact of silence that shrouded the whole country. As in Hitler's Germany, anyone who spoke out against the outrageous unlawful activities became the next victim, kidnapped and disappeared. The powerful Catholic Church went along with this state of affairs, except for a few courageous individuals whose bravery cost them their lives.

I was living in Tucumán, a province teeming with informants for the armed forces and dozens of clandestine detention centers. The reward for turning in neighbors, friends, family members, or acquaintances—one of the absolutely lowest things a human being can stoop to—was a state job or an array of other benefits. It was dangerous not to be aligned with the political right and thus to stand out from the flock of people who saw, heard, and said nothing. All of us were subject to a national system of intelligence that maintained endless files on everyone even remotely suspected of thinking differently.

In the midst of all that, I grew up, finished high school, and started college, all the while loving, working, making plans, singing, and crying—especially crying. I cried a lot because of my sense of helplessness and inability to do anything for the thousands of victims I met, heard, and watched as they wandered from place to place throughout the country seeking justice.

Then I decided that I could indeed do something: I could refuse to forget. I could hold in my memory all the details of these aberrations, so that one day in the future I might at least recount them to my own children.

Many years passed. The dictatorship ended and civil governments followed, but the power still held by the military weakened those presidencies. Indeed, two military uprisings had the effect of holding subsequent civil governments hostage. The unforgettable trials of the military junta under President Raúl Alfonsín were followed by laws that called for a national forgetting, and provided pardon and impunity to those responsible for the events of the late seventies and early eighties.

One day, more than twenty-five years after that March of 1976, this novel burst forth, surging up from my deepest being, where it had been stored in memories. It had remained there, suspended, as if floating on the breeze like an old piece of paper that refuses to be torn to tatters. Or perhaps I had already written this novel to myself, and that is why the characters, landscapes, and voices came to me with such speed and clarity that it was like a dream. Here are lodged the unfulfilled longings and deep pain for my country that, as I began to write, I suddenly realized just how much I love.

Gloria Lisé

Viditay, ya me voy
de los pagos del Tucumán,
en el Aconquija viene clareando
vidita, nunca te he de olvidar.

Viditay, triste está
suspirando mi corazón,
y con el pañuelo te voy diciendo
paloma, vidita, adiós, adiós.

Darling of my life, I am leaving
the region of Tucumán.
On Aconquija day is dawning;
My life's darling, I will never forget you.

Darling of my life, my heart is sighing
Sadly, and with my handkerchief
I am saying, Dove, Darling,
My life, good-bye, good-bye.

"Viene clareando" by Atahualpa Yupanqui[1]

1　A Pig's Head

THEY THREW HIM OFF a balcony at the headquarters of the
Tucumán Federation of Sugar Cane Workers. It was Atilio
Sandoval who exploded down on the sidewalk of General
Paz Street that hot night, a Tucumán night with a moon like
cheese, and fans, and cats on the roofs. On that night, unlike
the suffocating heat already giving way to the cooling winds of
fall, Atilio Sandoval, plainly and simply, did not give way, but
rather faced death, wearing it like a poncho.

It was March 23, 1976, and nothing would ever be the
same.

They killed him, and just like that, there he lay, on the
ground, dead, changed into a mere thing. Berta looked at his
shattered head, and before his blood could start stinking like
the slaughterhouse, she, who knew him so well, did the same as
everybody else in the vicinity: she pretended she had not seen
him and making sure her face did not give away her true feelings, she crossed the square. Opposite, the statue of Hipólito
Yrigoyen[2] stood with his back to the Palace of Justice, dressed
in the pocketless suit that portrayed him as the one president
who had not been a thief. He, with his back to the Palace of

Justice, was looking off in another direction. So was she, and more importantly, at that very moment she was promising herself that she would continue to do so from then on.

Atilio could not be offended now, nor would he have considered it an act of betrayal. He had lost, and they had crushed him just as they had sworn they would. Because of his beliefs, he had to fly off a balcony, leaving behind Tucumán, the ideals of social justice, Berta's love and embraces, and her body that had sat on that very sidewalk, listening to him address the masses from that very balcony. Yes, it was true: he had a weakness for balconies, for he was a Peronist through and through.

From now on she would look away, and it would not matter any more because Atilio would not be there to judge her lack of commitment or courage, something he had at times cursed her for, even though he knew better than anybody that she was a woman of principle.

"I shit on the history that birthed you," she said under her breath.

It was not an appropriate way to say good-bye to him; these were not the final words that should have accompanied such a love story.

But angered by the little that remained of the man on the sidewalk, she felt like attacking him with her feet and her fists, planting powerful blows on his body and face, all the while asking:

"Why? Why didn't you listen to me, why didn't we get away when we still could, why didn't all I had given you matter enough, why did you just so stubbornly keep pursuing your damn ideal of justice? Don't you see that they sold you, they turned you in, almost certainly just as you said the Bolivians did to Che when you ranted about him starting a revolution in Bolivia that the people didn't want."

"For a pig's head, the peasants handed over the *comandante*," he had said. And now he was the one reduced to nothing more than a flattened, one-dimensional image, grotesque, ugly, faceless, silenced forever in the few seconds that Berta knew would go round and round in her head through all the stories to follow. Now she simply had to escape, and make sure that nobody would suspect she was on the run.

She reacted as quickly as a cat in the middle of a fall. It was time to come up with unexpected visits to unknown family members, with scholarships, jobs, or commitments in far-away places. She had to leave Tucumán as quickly as she could. The last barrier had been broken, and now any and everything might happen. It was urgent: alert others, pack, waste no time on good-byes that no longer had any meaning, and look for a place in the world where she could just look off in another direction, like the Yrigoyen statue.

Like him, she had no need for pockets or huge suitcases, fashionable clothing, books, or her guitar. The time for silent screams was on its way, and the music would be locked up in her closet, along with those dresses she would not be wearing any more that would be packed away in mothballs, kept that way in hope that at some point her body would revert to what it had been and would welcome them, the dresses that would slip down over her up-stretched arms, grateful to become part of a life again.

2 The Ring

MOTHER, I AM ON MY WAY. I was able to buy a ticket to La Rioja, on a bus that takes me through Catamarca before it gets to where you grew up.

Last night, when I got home, I could see that you had already heard about it. So I just lowered my eyes and told you it was better for me to go away, surely for only a little while.

You were waiting for me, pale and more serious than ever, wordless, because you put more faith in action than words, and you never complain. You taught me that, and it is the way we will always be.

You didn't say a word to me; you just came to me after a little while with that handful of bills, all wrapped up carefully, Mother, because that is also the way you are, you are a Riera, introverted, wrapped into yourself, a pure Riojan. You gave me your pension, and I know that was all the money you have, and your blue bag, the canvas one that you get out only when you go to the Virgen del Valle, to the hospital or clinic to give birth; it's the lucky one, you used to say.

"Get going, child. You will find something. Go as far as you can and then get word to me of how you are doing."

On my way home, I'd heard they had taken Mauro Sandoval, Atilio's brother, the one who was head of the teachers' union, and everybody assumed he would turn up dead somewhere. Because of these two tragedies in the same family on the same night, people were praying for the mother and petitioning whichever saint had the responsibility to help in situations such as this.

I could not look you squarely in the eye, for I was not the daughter you had dreamed of. I was guilty; I had failed both myself and you. Now I was leaving you alone with all my brothers; leaving you, who had dreamed that I would be a doctor, a physician, paying you back for all your sleepless nights. Instead, I was going away like a thief, shaming and frightening you. You had to keep the door half-closed and let me know when the coast was clear so that no one would see me leave.

I know you had hoped I would leave all dressed in white for my wedding, the white wedding you never had, or as a doctor leaving to go and heal people and contribute to the country's progress. I couldn't deliver all that to you, Mother; I tried but failed, and now with the dawn so near there was no time to try to fix anything. I simply had to flee to try to save my skin and get through the night, which had to be the worst one of my life, Mother.

I don't know what I put in the blue bag—a rice tortilla you made me, the first tangerines of the season, and an apple, something you had always put in my school lunch. So, Mother, yet again you sent me off to face life with an apple; "an apple a day keeps the doctor away" was the saying you repeated, but

I was not hungry and thought I never would be again, and I don't remember if I even thanked you for all of it.

I debated whether to take my university notebook, unsure whether it would be dangerous or come in handy at some point, because at that stage it was not clear how things would turn out. I decided to take it and I kept it hidden in that extra seam in the bottom of the bag just in case they searched me.

We didn't say good-bye. I just lowered my head, the way I did when you scolded me as a little girl. I waited for you to complain for once in your life about this child, or shed a tear of anger, or slap me for loving Atilio so much and not listening to you. But no, Mother, instead of that, you tenderly made the sign of the cross on my forehead, like in a christening, and you told me:

"Never forget, daughter, that when you were born I gave you into the protection of the Virgin and San Nicolás of Bari. Your mother is right here, but the guardian angel is going with you to take care of you for me. Remember that wherever you go, if you give with one hand, God will bless you with two, and that you are named Berta Cristina because I consecrated you to Christ. So whenever you see a Sacred Heart, know it is your mother's heart praying for you, and if you bow you will show respect to your mother and to the Mother of God."

I left then without dragging things out or making any noise because the boys were asleep. I left you, alone, surrounded by all the religious images you filled the house with, and the frying pan that I hadn't washed because I didn't have time. I left with my university notebook, where they had written my grade, the grade you wanted: "Anatomy: passed with excellence, nine." I left you with my textbooks that you were still paying for. At the door, we just looked at each other.

All I could think of to tell you was:

"Don't forget to take your medicine, Mother."

And your eyes stayed with me, your eyes full of truth. Your eyes of farewell, of good-bye forever, eyes that didn't try to hide anything, because we both knew that you were ill, terminally ill, and that I wanted to take care of you but instead I was leaving, and you didn't even hold it against me. Your eyes told me that we would never see each other again.

I am now on the bus, in the early dawn on March 24, and I see the orchards full of oranges, lemons, grapefruit, and tangerines. It is harvest time. The sugar cane is green, Tucumán is green, dark green, maddeningly green, a green so intense that it seems to be exploding with life. So I think about Atilio, who will never again hold a sour orange in his hands, never again be able to tell me how the workers and students used to pick the fruit off the trees on the square to throw at the parading soldiers, or at the old guys so they would fall off their horses during the demonstrations. Atilio will never again be able to pluck an orange and smell the sweet aroma of its skin and tell me to make orange candy, and that if I don't know how, to learn and not be an ignoramus.

I slept a few minutes and saw your hands, Mother. Now you have the hands of an old woman and you are wearing the ring that was my grandfather's, Don Celestino Riera's, the one you put on just as your own mother did when her husband died, the one he had put on his own hand when he buried his mother. I see the ring on your finger, and I wake up and see the sun rising over Santiago del Estero. I am angry about all that has happened to me and to you, and I promise you, Mother, that I am going to live so that I, too, can put on that ring; that you are going to die an old woman and I will too; that some day I will return to Tucumán, and you will be proud of this successful daughter you have. I will close your eyes and you will rest in peace, and I will live in peace, because I am the daughter of your love and your pride, the fruit of your haughtiness. I will wear the Riera ring, our only fortune, because I will make a place for that angel you believe in, that one known by only you and three old ladies who pray with you: the guardian angel, who will take care of me, because I will let it take care of me, because that is what you want.

We will go on living, I swear this to you.

❸ A World Within a World

CONTRASTING MELODIES could be heard around the barrio of Matadero, the melodies of many people arriving from other parts looking for work in Tucumán or just passing through because of the railroad, the markets, and the possibility of menial part-time jobs in machinery and manufacturing. The place Berta was leaving was a place to start over for other people, not because it was a good place, but simply because it seemed not as bad as what they were trying to leave behind.

The Matadero slaughterhouse was fired up day and night, but by late afternoon, the chimney was spewing a bright fire that roared death and life. Livestock were headed to slaughter and workers to barely eke out a living. It was like a huge factory, an accepted hell, with the killers dressed in white from head to toe. The area was surrounded by shady money dealers and flanked by streets scarred by hundreds of carts waiting for the processed beef and the offal . . . carts that, as they traveled the bumps and curves, dripped tepid blood all over the neighborhood.

There were eating places, butcher shops, blacksmiths, and general merchandise stores where rural people stocked up.

These were people who wore sandals and narrow-brimmed hats, who drank wine by the liter; hard, gruff, fun-loving people who lived by the knife and horse or drove carts drawn by beasts with harnesses decked out with long leather ribbons, bejeweled with large tacks that gleamed in the early morning comings and goings or shone brightly in the midday sun that was so unhealthy for humans and animals. These people traveled from the first twinkle of a star to the first rays of dawn without complaining of the cold or the heat, a heat that could not be exaggerated. They came from the surrounding areas and from far away, bringing cattle and then carrying away the meat. They mingled with the coal carts coming from Santiago del Estero and the sugarcane carts that, in harvest season, spilled green cane that had been haphazardly and hastily loaded because of the clinging earth and the limited time set aside for milling; it was accepted that part of the cane, so wearily packed, would fall and rot along the roadways.

Along with the laborers came farm workers, the owners of small farms, truck drivers, card and dice players, other gamesters, vagrants, drunks, and all kinds of scoundrels. Some people seemed dark; others seemed light, because they lacked depth or complications, and their lives had already been sapped by the simple but precarious matter of day-to-day survival, which was no small matter. There were heavy smokers, who ate stews or empanadas at eight in the morning because for them that was already past midday, people with pasts full of deeds with knives, who didn't notice the smell of blood because they lived in it. And camps of gypsies who periodically settled in the area; to the neighbors who let them have access to water, they gave hope for travel, mystery, and gardens, because in the colorful blankets that they stretched over their tents and cars grew the only flowers in that whole vast brown neighborhood.

It was a world within another world, ignored by the police, on the outskirts of the city. Farther in was the Bridge of Sighs, full of stories about suicide for love, ghost sweethearts, hangings, countless acts of revenge or debt settlement, deaths inspired by every possible motive; and from time to time the train that crossed over the bridge knocked off a little bit more of its railings.

The neighborhood came to an end up on Juan B. Justo Avenue, where respectable Tucumán began, the part still known as "the pearl of the north." There was a neighborhood of good houses, named Bishop Piedra Buena in honor of a pro-independence priest, and the Salí River ran below, where the vegetation began to thin out until the desert took over at Santiago del Estero.

The trains marked the hours of the day, and children watched for them coming in from the south and played on the tracks, in the shadow of so many tragedies. Passengers would gather at the windows of the cars moving very slowly as they approached the San Miguel station and stare at the locals, who would in turn stare back. The passengers were people from the south, or *porteños* (from Buenos Aires), and northerners who were returning home, some with an arrogant manner from having traveled beyond the interior, and others with eyes showing defeat or gratitude for being able to come back.

The children could make a few pesos begging or selling biscuits or nougat prepared at home, all dry and tasteless. They asked for money from passengers at the end of their journey, who, precisely because their trip was over, did not feel they had to hang on to all their coins or did not worry that it was a waste to be charitable to the children of Matadero running alongside the train. Indeed, the visitors thought it might even bring them good luck, there where the countryside and the country estates of Tucumán, blooming with orange blossoms, gave way to poverty and misery. These were children whose parents were caught in the closing of plants and factories, whose families were piling up in a conglomeration of dark, rundown, ugly, brutal barrios.

It was in that world, among those people, that Doña Amalia del Valle Riera had found a house in Villa 9 de Julio shortly after the death of her husband. Berta was already fifteen, sheltered from all that Matadero was and stood for because her mother had made up her mind that this daughter was only passing through, that she would be a lady, one on the inside rather than the outside, or even better, a "Doctor." And each time Berta tried to play with the children of the neighborhood, her mother took her inside to her books and closing the door behind her, said:

"Remember, you are not one of those people. You are a Rojas del Pino."

4 This is My Family

IT IS MARCH 24. My mother's name is Amalia del Valle Riera, and my father was Manual Rojas del Pino, son of Alfonso the writer. I have four younger brothers: Carlos Alberto, Sergio Daniel, and the twins Juan José and Juan María. I was born in San Miguel de Tucumán on June 20, 1955, and they named me Berta Cristina; Berta for my father's godmother, and Cristina because that is what my mother chose. I am a medical student and have passed all the courses in the third year. I am leaving Tucumán because it's better for me to go away, because I had a lover and he died, because I am in great pain, because I need to work, because I have to help my mother who can barely support my brothers with her various jobs. My father left us when he was old. He became very sick, dying in my mother's arms as he received the last rites from the religion he never believed in but did respect, because he respected my mother and did not want to cross her, a devout Catholic. They finally got married after his first wife died, and then he gave us his last name, but he had always provided for us and never abandoned my mother, whom he treated as his real wife all along.

I have no connection with the Rojas del Pino family, as they have not wanted to have anything to do with us; my grandmother, Doña Lucinda, made sure while she was alive and healthy and my father, too, that we never set foot in her house, for we were children of sin, her son's bastard offspring. Well, my mother refused to accept that kind of treatment and thus did not take us to see her, not even the night when Doña Lucinda sent for us, to meet us, request our forgiveness, and give us a grandmother's blessing. She was dying and did not want to take with her to the next world the sin of ungodliness and lack of compassion that the priest rubbed her nose in during her last confession when he told her in no uncertain terms to settle all of that before she died. He was a new priest; the regular one had never considered it urgent. This priest was one of those who did not wear a cassock and went around saying that if Christ were to return today he would undoubtedly settle in a poor neighborhood, possibly even in Tucumán, or with the woodcutters of a factory, because those are his sheep, his brothers and sisters, the poorest of the poor and the most afflicted.

Doña Lucinda's employees came by car to summon us, in a hurry, saying that she was dying and that we should go immediately because that was what she had ordered. All of us children were waiting in the black convertible, all shiny under the streetlight, when my mother, furious and bristling like a lioness, without her glasses or shoes, hair uncombed, with her robe barely on, made us climb out of the car, shouting for us to get back into the house, and yelled at the driver at the top of her lungs so that all the neighbors could hear:

"Tell that old lady who threw me out of her house with my baby fifteen years ago, screaming at her son to 'get that garbage out of here,' to just take her sin with her and pay for it, just as I will take my own, and that I do not forgive her and that I curse her, and that we will meet again in hell, and may the Host burn in her mouth before I give, show, or take her my children. May she die a hundred times and give me the pleasure of spitting on her grave . . . bah . . . I shit on her and on the mother that bore her."

I was fifteen then and when I heard that, I understood things no one had ever told me. My father had died only a few months earlier, after suffering all kinds of indignities that completely undermined him.

We were living in the Villa, where my mother worked taking care of sick people at night, giving them shots, checking on those in the neighborhood with high blood pressure, as well as preparing food, especially empanadas and *maicenas*, and even helping Doña Carmen the seamstress when she had too much work. She used to say that she was the woman of a thousand jobs because my father's pension just didn't cover everything. We moved to Matadero because they threw us out of our house in the center of town. Most of the people there were on the fringes of society waiting and hoping to be land owners someday, whereas my mother, a widow at thirty-one, with five children and no relatives or friends to depend on in the area, was just trying to make a living. She had to create her own sense of dignity, because, as she taught me, in this life, "Nobody gives you anything, you have to earn it all on your own, even more so if you are a woman."

She was proud that her children always had something to wear on their feet and a clean school uniform.

"That is what you have a mother for," she told me.

There was no way we were going to be like the other children of the neighborhood; it was for that very purpose that she had two arms and a back as strong as a bull.

I went to Sarmiento School, a branch of the University, and graduated from there with a gold medal. My mother had decided long ago that I would not follow in her footsteps and therefore she never allowed me to work and always insisted that I bring home the highest grades. The sixth grade, which was as far as she got in La Rioja, had been enough to convince her that ours was the land of opportunity, savings, and progress all rooted in study and work, and that sacrifice brings reward, no question about it, and that a degree is now and forever the most important thing a child from poor neighborhoods or rural areas could ever acquire, and that the poor are poor primarily because they are tramps and drunks. For all those reasons in the elections she was voting for Manrique, a military man, a respectable man.

My future had already been decided; I would be a doctor.

Thus it was that I enrolled in the School of Medicine and studied so conscientiously. I studied because I loved studying and I loved my mother more than anything else, along with medicine. And I had only watched from the sidelines the political fervor and activity taking place in Tucumán. I didn't read or talk about politics. I had my opinions but I never joined any party, society, or movement; I didn't participate in movements based on putting ideas into practice the way almost all my friends and companions did. All I ever concentrated on was becoming a doctor, because there was never enough food to go around at home so I didn't have the luxury of getting behind in my studies or allowing my mother to continue to support me past the time when I could and should have finished and begun working to help provide for my brothers. People my age, as a general rule, have lofty, mostly good intentions, and new ideas that keep them all wrapped up in getting themselves and the rest of the world ready for the changes to come, and because of that many of them quit studying or working, or work even harder, making huge changes in their lives, and this takes up all their energy and hope. Atilio was like that, and sometimes we argued because I just couldn't understand, until he had that accident and died before we were able to reach an agreement about all those things that were so important to him.

I had other, more pressing dreams to realize, regardless of whether they were originally my mother's or my own, and I was preparing myself to be able to make a difference in the world later, armed with the thing I believed in most—a profession that enables you to save lives and alleviate pain. And still, even before I could actually dedicate myself to that, I would have to contribute to the needs of my own family.

My father had never had dreams for me. He had given up everything in September of 1955, shortly after I was born.

This is who I am, my life history, a life explained by what has happened to other people, my life that belongs to my father, mother, grandparents, and to the man I lost. And I am also others, made up of other hatreds, shames, and passions that are not really mine, but that are part of me. Maybe it was all those reasons that led me, on a night when I could have headed to almost any destination, to choose as I did—which is why I am on this bus that has passed through Santiago and is now turning toward Catamarca, on my way to La Rioja.

I don't know them, but I am headed to the home of the Rieras.

I will tell them this story, ask for advice and lodging, and look for whatever trace might still remain in the old family home of that arrogant, intelligent, and indomitable girl who became my mother, and whether the balcony is still there where my father fell in love with her, or the antique lock on the door where they passed their messages, love letters as well as plans for running away together—he a grown married man from a Tucumán family, she a child of sixteen from a Rioja family.

I will not ask anybody to forgive what my mother and father did.

It is March 24, I am twenty years old, and I am going to my roots.

⑤ Listening to the Radio

THE BUS PULLED INTO Ciudad Loreto, which was nothing more than a group of houses that had kept the name given to it by its first settlers, people who had had to face a harsh climate, whose droughts dashed any hope for industry, gardens, or progress that might justify the name "city." It was well past daybreak and the driver wanted his breakfast. The sound of a radio brought together drivers, passengers, villagers, and waiters in the snack bar that also served as the bus terminal. A military march was playing. The public was then informed that a military junta had taken over the government, that Mrs. María Estela Martínez de Perón, known as Isabel, was no longer President of the Argentine Republic, and that the three top men of the three respective military branches were now governing the country in the name of national reconstruction. We were told that all across the nation martial law was in effect; all residents were ordered to cooperate fully and obediently with any orders issued from the military authority from then on.

The radio resumed its military music and then began to broadcast various communiqués, always identified as "from the ruling military junta" and read by a powerful male voice whose diction, volume, and style reminded people of other coups, which had been announced with other similar decrees that no longer surprised anybody.

Some people were delighted and were yelling, "At last!" and, "It's about time!"

They thought this one would be just like all the others and that the military would put things in order the way it had been doing from time to time for at least forty-five years. Once again the black lists would appear: of people, the press, and songs. There would be raids, political prisoners would be taken, congress abolished, political parties outlawed, and some provinces taken over—but not much beyond all that, and in several months or perhaps a few years the next elections would be announced. General Videla,[3] considered by the press as one of the "good" military men, would have the support of the traditional non-Peronist parties and even of some progressive and moderate leftist sectors calling for a "military-civil government." The public would be in general agreement with that because everything would be taking its normal course, for the glory and well-being of the Argentine people, a people every group or party claimed to represent.

Yes, they thought, this would be one more chapter, just like the others, in Argentina's recent history, a stark chapter referred to in school textbooks as *la alternancia* (the alternation), the series of civil governments interrupted by military coups beginning in 1930. At Sarmiento School, they called it "the sausage," a segment of history that the teachers tended to ignore until the very last days of class. The section devoted to that period barely even gave the names of the presidents that the portrait gallery hastily presented, in which each one was pictured with the presidential seal, dates of birth, death, and years of presidency, and party affiliation if there was one. It was a way of thinking that said that particular piece of history was worth just about ten coins or at most one paper bill, blue and worthless except to buy a single pack of unfiltered cigarettes. It always began when General José Uriburu overthrew the elected government of Hipólito Yrigoyen, described even by his own men in the official texts as an old, washed-up has-been; from that point on everything was presented in the briefest paragraphs up until Perón.

Why were some governments considered military and some civil? Why were some civil presidents addressed as General and dressed in uniform such as Perón? It seemed that in the first case the military ruled directly and in the second it used force to control the result of elections. The difference was hard to understand and was just one of the many questions you couldn't ask in class, for your own and other people's sake, during a dictatorship. You could sometimes debate the answers to these questions behind closed doors with the few teachers who were brave enough to speak up in meetings whose main theme ended up being: who is the owner of the sausage-making machine?

A sausage period, in the nation known for its huge cold-storage plants.

"Alternation; taking turns," Berta pronounced under her breath when she heard the first comuniqué and, with eyes closed, saw those pages in the worn school textbook. But in her body and soul, she somehow knew that this time it would be different, because this history was no longer one out of a book but rather her own. It had begun with death, and Tucumán was becoming a cauldron of violence. Perón had died and all that was left were his speeches full of clichés repeated over and over and out of context. Nevertheless, this guaranteed that he would continue to exert his own particular influence on the present reality, that of the Montoneros,[4] the guerillas who had dedicated "their lives to Perón" and were now in hiding; that of the groups referring to themselves as "farther to the left than leftists" who were clearly anti-Peronists, which included grassroots groups with or without their own army; those who claimed to be Leninists, Castroites, Maoists, or Trotskyites; the most "orthodox" labor unionists; the "Iron Guard;" the Argentine Anti-Communist Alliance, or Triple A[5]; radicals, armed or unarmed; Communists accused of being right wing or bourgeois; local parties and small alliances snuffed out in the daily armed activities supposedly carried out for the good of the people and progress by groups banded together in the name of the poor or by those standing for such abstract ideals as goodness, Christian or Western morality; and others, who defended God, country, and home, even as they offended God in every way possible, violating all the laws of this land called a nation, and destroying the homes of both rich and poor, of both intellectuals and simple folk, denying the right to speak or to listen even to those who in the name of God, country, and home might come begging for reasonableness and the most basic respect for life; all in agreement that they only wanted to save the country from some imperialist power or conspiracy that some maintained dated back to five thousand years before Christ was born.[6]

And even Peronists came in many colors: genuine Peronists; historic Peronists; neighborhood Peronists; Peronists for liberation, for the Peronist party, for the *justicialista* or social welfare movement; Peronists with Perón; Peronists with Evita or without Perón; Peronists calling for a socialist country; nationalist and anti-Communist Peronists; grassroots Peronists; and basic-unity Peronists. And still more: civil groups, military groups, paramilitaries, and parapolice. And all kinds of "fronts:" for the unity of the movements, for the unity of the Peronists, against and for the government, laborer and union fronts, the latest fronts, those of certain leanings, of parties, of anyone offended by anything. And in each faction or party, there were true believers and traitors, martyrs and those condemned, some who judged in their own courts, and some with jails run by the people or by drunkards. Each in its own way claimed to have the answer and serve as the necessary cleansing element, representing the one and only true voice of the people, of justice, of the country, and to be the only hope for salvation if only the rest would accept and follow their group's beliefs.

Almost all the groups denounced the government's failure and the inefficiency of its institutions and of democracy, the same way people had lost respect for and confidence in the courts that were corrupt and thus not living up to the traditional idea of justice—that is, to each his or her just reward or punishment. So the nights were filled with senseless violence, senseless unless one considered the past twenty years or more of alliances and exclusions, exiles and returns, amnesties and agreements among the protagonists in Argentine political life, not to mention the various parties and their dissolution plus

the power of the military and the Church. With such a historical view, one might understand how the country's shroud had
been woven for a whole generation.

Little by little, people were becoming accustomed to living
in shock and horror, and their indignation gave way to a kind
of fatalism formed in a period that felt like forever but really
wasn't all that long, during which a silent tragedy was unfolding, a tragedy in which nobody was listening to anybody else
or understanding what they were saying, because the shared
meaning of the most basic words had been lost. Everything
was defined by action, and being a man of action, or of weapons, which was almost the same thing, became the new para-
digm for many, many people.

For all those reasons, even before the coup, at nightfall a
different Tucumán came to life, where civilians patrolled as
if they were soldiers in combat, soldiers as if they were delin-
quents, all of them carrying "arms" against a government that
had made use of all the actors in this opera in red and black,
and in which they all understood and practiced justice, believing that if there was any moral cause it was their own, and that
it was definitely a "legitimate defense" to arm oneself against a
weak and corrupt democratic government, because it had lost
legitimacy. Whoever opposed it was okay. And in the middle
of all this drama, the power of the state, the judicial system, and
congress all but vanished, and the political parties and unions
were at a complete loss and powerless, just waiting for somebody, anybody, to fix the mess.

Once again Tucumán found itself to be the nation's navel,
condemned to repeat its history in which it uttered the first

cry, felt the first pain, became the site of the first experimental efforts and projects of struggle and social change of all kinds. Tucumán: cradle of three presidents, of the *Tucumanazo* uprising,[7] of the guerilla movement in the mountains, and the defeat of the same. TUCUMÁN, THE GRAVE OF SUBVERSION was the slogan displayed on the bright poster Governor Bussi[8] hung in the plaza of South America's biggest park during the centennial celebration, because he was a major enforcer of *Operativo Independencia*. His stated purpose was the extermination of the guerillas, ordered by the President, despite the fact that the movement had already been completely wiped out.

Berta understood deep within her that what was going on now made this a period quite different from the coups and civilian governments of the past, with their varying degrees of bloodiness and permissiveness. Already too many graves had been dug, too many wakes held, and too much black ink used in the photographs printed in *La Gaceta* documenting attacks, revenge, and retaliation, specific convictions, bombed vehicles, dismembered soldiers, humiliated soldiers, humiliated politicians, flags at half mast, heartfelt tributes, tactical errors, military failures, political successes, holidays, strikes, repression of the strikes, civil and military burials, marches, fist fights, and armed confrontations. There had already been many years of ungodliness, injustice, and senselessness before March 24, 1976.

Thus, on this morning, nobody was feeling sorry for Isabelita; the "Female Fool"'s game of playing President had ended. Both the "Old Man" and his minister for social welfare, the so-called "Wizard," were gone. The horizon was clearing. It seemed that Peronism had finally come to an end and that from now on to call yourself a Peronist would be to say a bad word.

"I wonder what will be on the front page of today's *La Gaceta*," thought Berta. "The headlines will probably declare this the beginning of a happy new era." The paper would surely argue that the state, no matter how bad or short-lived a particular government might be, would not attack its own people. Regardless of who these three military officers were, they would not harm the country but simply move it forward with a little of their characteristic discipline and morality. The populace would just have to be content—after all, it was for their own good. That was the purpose of newspapers such as *La Gaceta*—to help shape public opinion in Tucumán.

But sitting there, in the middle of nowhere at the Ciudad Loreto stop, Berta's thoughts were focused only on getting farther away, on leaving Tucumán and its outlying areas, on arriving at a place that had nothing whatsoever to do with what she had left behind, and on creating for herself a new identity and purpose that would explain her presence elsewhere. Even though she had impulsively chosen La Rioja for the immediate present, it might easily be somewhere else tomorrow.

Throughout the trip, at the stops along the way, she had seen trucks carrying soldiers armed for combat, tanks waiting on the outskirts of cities, military conscripts grouped together at the edges of the towns, helicopters and combat planes crisscrossing the skies. Some of the passengers' faces betrayed deep worry whereas others' shone with exultation or even euphoria.

The latter, without the slightest trace of fear, were discussing the return of order and decency to Argentina, the death of the dog and the end of his rabid attacks, and the fact that people would once again live in peace, something they never should have lost at the hands of "corrupt and lying politicians."

Back at the wheel and on the road, the driver turned on the radio, and Berta checked to make sure she had her blue canvas bag. A tango started to play and it seemed to her as if the melody pinned her to the seat and carved a deep fissure in her heart, for Jorge Sobral was singing "*Fuimos*/ What We Were," accompanied by a single violin:

We were the hope
That never arrives or materializes,
That cannot glimpse its tame afternoon,
We were the traveler who, asking for nothing,
Neither praying nor crying,
Began dying.

And she pressed her lips together, because never again would she talk about what was or what "we were," for there would never be a "we" again, with anybody; at least not unless the angel appeared, the one her mother had told her about, the one that would wake her up and convince her that it had all been a dream, just a bad nightmare; that Tucumán was drunk with orange blossoms and that Atilio was there, just as he had been every afternoon, waiting for her at the end of classes in the Central Plaza. She would let her hair loose and shake it from side to side to make it seem longer and he would simply say, "Sweetheart!"

But the bus just kept on swallowing up the road. Berta made a bitter face at her reflection in the window and said to herself: "You poor old thing!"

6 Flowers

LA RIOJA IS THE SAME in spring, summer, and fall, but in
winter something different starts to happen because San Nicolás Day is celebrated in June, when the cathedral is decorated
with paper flowers, and the crowned saint and the Virgin are
carried in procession. Perhaps because these are tithing days,
it seems less dry and less windy. The forecast may predict cool
and rainy weather, but what usually happens is that it is the
hottest and most oppressive that anyone can remember and
everybody says, "how the weather has changed," or "it used to
be cooler," and "it's not fit for living now," and "now that we
have the levees, it's worse."

That's about all I know about the region and its main city,
named Todos los Santos de la Nueva Rioja, located at the foot
of the Sierras de Velasco, told to me by my mother, who hardly
told me anything, maybe because she and my father believed
that talking about the past was something weak people do.
"Talking about oneself is stooping to the low level of those
lacking character or will, complainers, who err due to their lack
of humility" is the way my mother sometimes put it, possibly

paraphrasing her teachers, the nuns—who in educating her, only made her more rebellious—or her "old folks," which was what she called her grandparents.

I have reached the terminal and gotten off the bus that is going on to Cuyo. I am in an unsophisticated city with low, carefully arranged houses that, if not for the few colonial structures interspersed among them, would seem to have been founded in this century. Here everything is small—the gardens, people, and pavements—and I walk along, trying to make myself smaller. It is early evening and I see television sets turned on, children playing in the yards, and teachers in white uniforms on their way home.

I look for Asunción Street and ask an old man, who is sitting on a cane-bottom chair leaning against the wall of a house, for the Riera family home, and he tells me, pointing: "It's on the next block, see, on the corner, where you'll see a big door, there where it turns into a dirt road." He has answered me with a melodious accent I recognize, that kind of flirtatious, sweet tone that my mother used when she was putting us to bed.

I get to the double doors, which are ajar, and notice that they are antique, like everything else about the centuries-old house. Inside I can see a patio with a *jacaranda* tree in the center and red pots full of ferns, begonias, geraniums, and other flowers I don't recognize, and a birdcage with canaries and cardinals behind the grate, separating the hall from the entrance. I look above the door and I see the words BLESS THIS HOME in black and white on a piece of worn brass held in the arms of Jesus the Good Shepherd. I stand there taking it all in, and gradually I realize that there are people inside the houses across the street and on both sides, people I do not see but who see me, who are watching me—old men and women, observing quietly, making sure they don't miss anything.

Then I notice that two eyes inside the house are also gazing at me through glasses with thick black frames, behind which is a small face. It disappears. I keep looking at the front of the house and notice that the doorknocker, made of iron, has the shape of a delicate lady's hand wearing a ring. I hesitate to knock with it and see that the keyhole of the door is enormous, and I think the keys must be like the ones in museums, and that through that keyhole anything could pass, including a love story.

At that moment the woman in the glasses who has been watching me from inside the house appears. She is so short and fat that she looks to me like an erect little frog standing on two legs, her little arms at her sides like parentheses around a body that is wobbling, because nature wanted it to be circular. The legs are also parentheses through which I can still glimpse the house and the patio with plants in red pots. She waits quietly in the doorway, and I am standing in front of the door to her house and I no longer know where I am, how old I am, or even who I am, for I would rather be somebody else somewhere else, and I look down at her because she comes only to a little above my navel and see she is examining me curiously.

I shift my gaze to the small garden in front of the house so that she can inspect me in peace, and I see on my left a flowering calla lily. Indeed, there are many white, moist, fresh lilies, rising tall and dignified in the middle of the desert, triumphant over barren earth where generations have swept and sprinkled water in the afternoon because of the dusty winds that begin in March and never seem to stop. I see the lilies and smell the water falling on them from a dripping spigot. I think that I have never liked those flowers because they are a symbol of death, like carnations, and because lilies don't grow in Tucumán, and my mother doesn't like them either, because the last ones we saw were at my father's wake so they are flowers of sadness. But now that I am looking at them, so white and beautiful, flowers like bunches of water that I want in my mouth, I realize that I am thirsty.

Thirsty, and it is the first time I have felt anything in the three days since I left home; I realize that during those days I have not felt the heat or cold or the wind or gotten sleepy at siesta time. I have not felt pain or fear or anxiety, I have not been hungry for anything, not even for justice, love, or flowers. And now I see the water and I want it, I need it so I can go on living, and I envy those lilies.

The woman says to me, "You must be the daughter of my sister Amalia."

I am so weak I can barely stay standing in my shoes, inside the clothes that have turned to paper. Still, I am determined to hang on to the blue bag in my hand. And I answer:

"Yes."

It is a yes to myself, because I no longer have the breath to get anything out of me; my voice swallows the word, swallows me into myself; it is a "yes" that goes unheard.

I am still looking at the lilies and I feel, suddenly *feel* everything: that I need water to live, to be brave, to be able to take that one step that will carry my body over the threshold to somewhere else. I, who am strong, tall, and big, collapse and begin to cry, unable to stop, with sobs the woman seems to understand immediately. She takes me inside the house and sits me down in a parlor, where I just keep on crying, unable to say a single word or to stop even though I try with all my might. She puts before me a heavy glass that seems as old as she is.

She tells me to drink. I am crying so hard that I cannot get down even a drop, because in order to live you not only have to want to but you also have to be able to, so I try and I choke and sob without ceasing in that parlor that smells of family, my family, my people, bones like mine, poverty like mine, words and signs and flower vases and photos, tablecloths and lap desks like mine, and I am at home and sobbing in front of the glass the woman has brought me, crying harder and harder so that I only barely manage to say thank you.

She leaves me alone, seated in an austere wooden chair where my great-great-grandparents must have found rest, me with my blue canvas bag resting on my knees; she goes out, leaving the door ajar so that I can cry in peace but not totally alone, and before she leaves, she makes a gesture to me as if saying:

"Relax in peace, you are welcome here."

I keep crying and prepare myself for a spell of weeping that will last hours, days, months, years, centuries, preparing to cry for the rest of my life, because I don't believe in angels, or in divine providence, I just barely believe in those proud lilies enjoying the water, and everything is dark.

It is night inside this parlor and I am aware that someone else has come into the house, someone with an old man's voice, who perhaps has overheard everything. I can make out the sound of cooking and smell the food frying, and she says to him, in that sweet voice of hers:

"For her to be crying like that, it has to be over a man."

7 The Photograph

THERE WERE FIVE SIBLINGS, three brothers and two sisters. The brothers and my mother, Amalia, looked a lot alike. They had the characteristic Inca face—a deep dark brown color—and they were tall, stout, and muscular. Their hair, jet black in their youth before turning prematurely gray, was thick and straight and they wore it combed back. All of them were nearsighted, with a slightly crooked gaze. Avelina, who was eleven years older than Amalia, had not inherited the height or the distinguished gait of her siblings, but she did get the skin color and became nearsighted at an early age. She owed her very life to science and incubators because without them she would not have survived her difficult birth.

This was a family of arrogant yet poor people, despite the land they had owned ever since the conquest. The only thing their land was good for was raising goats as hard and muscular as themselves. It was just a vast expanse of barren land, "desert" in the scornful words of my mother, the youngest. That is all they had, except for their pride based on who knows what. Maybe it simply emerged from that parlor where I was now sitting and where I had lost my composure, much to my surprise, for I too was a Riera, and a Rojas del Pino on top of that. I had the same last name as my aunts and uncles, and the same inexplicable haughtiness, the tendency to brag about being the opposite of meek, being a law unto ourselves, just because, because that's the way we were made. "The clothes tag in the selvage edge," was how it was described at home.

All the boys were named Tristán after their father's friend, Tristán Frías, who had done some really big favor for my grandfather. Although it was never clear to them exactly what he had done, it had to be important for, in honor of and gratitude toward him, not only was each son given his first name but he was also their godfather.

Tristán Nepomuceno, the oldest, was known as *el Negro*; Tristán Clímaco as Maco; and Tristán Javier, Javier—each one named for his own saint, because that is how Grandmother wanted it, not to mention that that was just the way it had always been done. The girls were born after the boys and Grandmother chose the names, names of heroines she liked: "Avelina" was for Avelina Hauser in *Castillos de los Riscos*, an ever repeating radio soap opera, and "Amalia" came from the novel by José Mármol.

The Riera brothers had beautiful voices and a talent for singing and playing guitar, and because of that they liked nightlife and formed a group, *Los Hermanos Tristán*, that performed folk music and tangos. They played guitars to accompany the *criollo* waltzes they sang and the gaucho poetry they recited—all of which led to more and more parties best suited to the single life. They did this, as my mother used to say, "because your grandmother brought them up wrong."

Yet all of them landed good jobs in the public sector: Tristán Nepomuceno as an administrative employee with the railroad, because he was long-winded and had good handwriting; Tristán Javier with the post office, a position he obtained through my father after Papa married my mother and made peace with her family; and Tristán Clímaco as a low-level administrator with the Provincial Police before he retired early and moved to Buenos Aires, after the grandparents died, where he married a widow.

They met my father in the early fifties when he regularly stayed out late to listen to the *peñas*.[9] He was a manager of government employees, sent by the politicos to Catamarca, La Rioja, Mendoza, San Juan, or wherever he was needed to promote the Peronist agenda. He ended up as Chief of Mail Services in Tucumán. When he was in La Rioja, he stayed in the Príncipe Hotel, where there was a restaurant and bar that my uncles often played in. That is how he got to know them. By that time he was over forty and had two almost fully grown sons living in Catamarca with his legal wife, who was several years older than he was. She was from a good family with a considerable inheritance in San Fernando.

He got my mother pregnant when she was sixteen, thus violating all the trust her brothers had shown him, and they ran away together. Her father, Don Celestino, gave her up for dead and made his wife wear mourning clothes and offer intercessory prayers for their daughter in the Requiem Mass. All the siblings, including Avelina, were punished because of what they knew but didn't tell, what they should have known but didn't, and simply what they failed to warn their parents about. It was only right that all of them had to suffer for the loss of family honor and of the most beautiful member of the Riera family—the incorrigible, unmanageable, and bold one who was my mother, who gave up her dream of being a pilot because she was pregnant with me. She left behind a letter in which she confessed everything and asked for respect for the man of her life, to whom she herself had lied about her age, and who was taking her away to be his woman and companion for the rest of their lives.

Nobody thought it would ever happen, but one day all of us went back to that house to visit. My mother, now married to my father, was more dazzling than Evita; I was dressed in white, including a lace cap; and my two younger brothers were wearing suits and ties. The twins were not yet born. We arrived by car because my father was still important and we were respectable people. My mother and father were good-looking and successful, and the way they acted gave the impression that they were saying, "Forgive what we did, but it was such a powerful love."

Grandfather Riera shook hands with my father as if he had been his life-long, dearly beloved son-in-law. My grandmother was content and cooked the whole time, or sat on the patio with the *jacaranda* tree and her daughters, all three talking together next to the cage of canaries and cardinals. Aunt Avelina hugged us to her breast.

And there on the wall is a picture of the whole family together, a photo taken of us on the patio: me in my white shoes on my father's knees; my brothers standing on either side of my mother; Avelina sitting on a big pillow to look taller; our grandfather with his mustache, in his rocking chair; our tiny grandmother dressed in black, holding a hand over her mouth because she was not used to having her picture taken, but smiling; and the Uncles Tristán standing in the back with their guitars; in this room, where the picture is hanging on a wall faded by the passing of time, in this house that we never came back to.

I don't remember that visit; my mother from time to time would tell me all about it, and I would imagine this place. And here I am trying to remember the story as I look at the photograph presiding over the parlor. I can see in my mind the pieces of crockery that shattered one day when my parents kicked aside all formality and convention, a time when I was already in the womb, the womb of this house, humid, in need of paint, with pictures of scenery that no longer exists, with time asleep on the walls, and with cordless guitars that went away already, because they had had their day.

8 Aunt Avelina

VERY LITTLE OF HER FACE could be seen because of her thick, heavy glasses, which made her look so ugly that she inspired sympathy, a bit like the bewitched toads in fairy tales that could change into princes at any moment, merely by being kissed by the right person. But Avelina did not admit to any physical defect and always thought of herself as an attractive and sensual woman, having been educated by the graphic novels that made their way to La Rioja. To be sure she got her hands on those, she was perfectly capable of lying, robbing, or blackmailing her brothers so they would buy them for her. Besides that source of self-confidence, there were her parents, the Rieras, who made it clear to her—even swore to her—that she was unique, a gift from God and the Virgin, and that others envied her for having a family that loved her so much.

Avelina had been premature, coming into the world at seven months, fully enveloped in a caul. The whole community had prayed and organized masses, processions, and penance ceremonies to save the little infant. Weighing less than two pounds, from the beginning she had shown her strong desire to exist and be a part of this world. Her parents cared for her as they would for a fine gem and all they wanted in return was that she survive. She did not turn out to be a miracle child in spite of the Virgin's mantle, but she did learn how to overcome timidity at a very young age. Short, stocky, chubby, and very bowlegged, she was known for her good humor, pleasant and optimistic temperament, and her passion for boleros, which the whole city was forced to listen to once her family acquired a record player, for she set it up on the sidewalk morning and afternoon, turned up to full volume.

When Amalia ran off, Tristán Nepomuceno had a chat with Grandfather that went something like this:

"Papa, don't you think you ought to be stricter with Avelina? What if the same thing happens with her as with Amalita?"

Grandfather Riera bit into his corn and anise cigar because he had ordered everybody not to mention Amalia's name ever again, and after spluttering several times, he asked his oldest son, in a very surprised voice:

"But . . . who is going to notice Avelina?"

"Don't be fooled, Papa, even she, just as she is, has her suitors."

The face of the old man, Don Celestino, contorted in rage; clearly, once more they were hiding things from him. How could this be possible? His daughters were simply hopeless! He was already removing his belt buckle to whip Avelina, when his son, fully expecting such a reaction, told him:

"Hold it, Old Man, Avelina doesn't even know anything yet. It's true that someone is interested in her, but he hasn't gotten up the courage to come to talk to you yet. I myself just found out."

Grandfather settled down again in the patio chair and felt the shade of the century-old *jacaranda* tree cool his head and at that very moment, just like in one of the novels my aunt devoured, the wind blew down a shower of flowers from the tree above him. His mustache splashed with those celestial announcements of spring, he asked in a calm voice who the man was who was asking and whether they ought to consider it.

"It's the Gringo, Old Man, my co-worker at the railroad, the engineer."

"Who? The crippled Gringo?" he asked, making a face of clear disgust.

"Well, Papa, we aren't going to be overly demanding in terms of Avelina, right? Besides, the Gringo is a widower and a hard worker."

The Gringo had entered the country on an Italian passport, coming to Argentina because his own city was no longer there, nor his family, all having been bombed during the war. An engineer, he had served in the army because he was drafted, like everybody else in his town, and the right foot he had lost when he stepped on a landmine was the least of his regrets because the war had also taken his wife, the most beautiful woman in Palermo, along with his five-year-old son.

The Gringo, who was in his midfifties, was hired by the railroad to work as an engineer in undesirable places, dynamiting openings for future bridges and roads, because in this country people were preparing for the future, something he liked. Besides, it was exciting to blow up hills and watch everything fly though the air, because here it was a game and they were creating straight lines and curves where nature had not provided them. He came back to life by setting off the biggest explosions and risking his life until the last second, and then dreaming at night in the camps set up in the deserts of La Rioja that he was putting the same bombs under the beds of the ones who had started the war. That way he could and did kill generals, governors, politicians, princes, aristocrats, and paupers, the well-educated and the ignorant—all those he considered responsible for destroying his world.

Every time he woke up, though, he realized he could never kill anyone, that he was incapable of committing any act of revenge, that in spite of the horrible things that had happened to him, some small part of him was still alive and allowed his heart in the late afternoons to sing Italian songs or tunes from this, his new country. With the final feverish blasts concluded, he soaked up every last drop of the sunset at the end of the day, and told the workers that the western sky was a person's reward for having worked hard all day. He could barely speak Spanish, but then he didn't really talk much anyway, he was a man who listened. He drank the strongest Rioja wine, and ate lots of beef, with bread and potatoes, even though his body had been sucked away by the cigarettes that never left his mouth during the day. He didn't cry about his unhappiness but rather shut it up inside him.

One day, when the Gringo was walking along Asunción Street, he saw a record player on the sidewalk outside number fifty-five that was sending through its speakers a wrenching and sweet bolero sung by Olga Guillot: "Kiss me, kiss me over and over." Looking inside, he saw the doors to the hall slightly open, ferns and a recently swept patio in the background, and off to the side beneath a dripping pipe, lush, thick, full-grown white lilies. They reminded him of the fountain in the plaza in his town, and a girl with fine, curly blond hair like a child's and perfect feet sitting beside that fountain, where water was splashing from a pitcher carried on the shoulder of a pagan god; and in the fountain were lilies that cooled and refreshed you simply because you looked at them, for it was summer, and she was waiting for him to tell him yes, that she loved him.

These flowers in La Rioja weren't the same kind, but they were a reminder that flowed through him, the familiar needle stabbing his chest whenever she appeared to him: the lilies on the altar the night they got married in Santa Rosalía. Her name had been Rosalía, and the saint had fulfilled her promise that she would get married.

The record player was playing so loudly that he assumed there must be a party going on inside the house, and the bolero reminded him of kissing—this man who had never kissed again because he had not been able to give his wife one last kiss, or his son, or his siblings, or his mother, who had died after he got to Argentina.

He just stood there, like someone admiring the garden, because he had not expected to find lilies in La Rioja and expected even less to hear of kisses in a house that seemed like it had a party going on but really only contained a little woman sitting down, calmly mending socks and drinking her *mate*, wearing glasses that covered half her face; a person so short that her legs dangled from the chair, legs that were keeping time to the bolero rhythm as if she were dancing. She looked up and the needle stuck her in her finger because the Gringo was a tall man with sky-colored eyes and lots of thick, graying blond hair, stiff as straw and combed back. He was skinny as a wire, and she studied him slowly to the beat of the dance that was an invitation to love, and she saw that the man was standing on one true leg while the other one ended in a cane covered with a buttoned shoe. She looked at the leg and understood everything, and he looked at the little woman with two legs that had never been squeezed close to a man's in dancing such a bolero, because she was, for sure, the ugliest girl in that less than attractive city.

At that moment the record ended, leaving them both staring at each other, and Avelina smiled a smile that came from deep within, from the wisdom and compassion she had inherited from all the women who preceded her, the Criollas, Spanish Galicians, and Indians, and some Turkish great-grandmother who had also contributed some blood to the family. It was the smile of a woman who knew what it was to be a woman and who liked it, who was made for love and was grateful for the little or lot that came her way, because she had known from the very beginning that someday the kiss that life had prepared for her would arrive.

She smiled at him, confident of herself, and she put down her darning and said to him, "If you like, I can play it again."

The Gringo tottered on his cane foot and mumbled something incomprehensible in the language of his country, perhaps asking to be excused. Avelina looked into his eyes, taking off her glasses as if she needed them only for sewing, so she could be clear, and insisted:

"Shall I play it again?"

"Yes," said the Gringo, using an excess of words.

Then Avelina got down from the chair and put the record on again and the Gringo just stood there. The two of them, looking at each other, openly and equally, discovered as easily as that—even as Miss Guillot was shaking the record player while demanding kisses from all of La Rioja—that they could go down the path of life together.

So Avelina got married and enjoyed very happy nights and days with her lame man, who never had been very healthy and whose kidneys, destroyed by the war, were just getting worse. The marriage lasted only ten years, because the Gringo died in his mid sixties, but he always loved his ugly wife who loved him like a prince. Although they never had children of their own, she kept a candle burning in front of the photo taken before the war, of the Gringo's now-dead little son in his mother's arms, and they told everybody with deep tenderness:

"We have our own little angel."

9 Her Body

BERTA SUDDENLY FELT it was time to leave that parlor, for her body was telling her she had to live, even though death was still lurking close by, from her right side all the way to as far as she could see. She had to live because she was a young Tucumana, with dark skin and dark brown eyes, whose hands and feet were so small and delicate that they contrasted delightfully with her tall stature; and because she was carrying with her in the bottom of her blue bag a university notebook— no matter that she was hiding it and hiding herself behind her dark straight hair and the thick glasses that slightly veiled her striking features. Those characteristics were enough, because it was March of a leap year, a leap year that, in its third month, like lightning, was rushing headlong to nowhere.

She realized that she was feeling and hearing her body because it had gotten far away from so much hatred and fear. Now she could allow herself the luxury of actually living in her body and in that way simply survive.

She looked for a mirror to see what remained of her face after all she had been through and found a little bit of glass in the cupboard. But before she managed, with great effort, to see her own reflection, she saw lots of little unmatched cups and glasses, a mix of antiques and everyday little ceramic dolls, faded good-luck elephants, a souvenir from Mar del Plata, "the happy city," and many mementoes from baptisms, first communions, weddings, and anniversaries. All were now faded and worn to yellowing reminders of happier times, and of children who today were grown men and women, sweethearts who were now grandparents. She felt tender toward the person who had kept all those things that nobody else was interested in and that were turning ugly and ridiculous with the passing of time. Who could that person be with such a nostalgic and careful touch? Surely a woman; her mother's sister. Then she looked at herself, noticing her eyes reddened from so much crying and her thick hair, messy like a dirty old broom. She also noticed that she too was getting a few gray hairs; in fact, they were pretty obvious. The Rieras turned gray early, and now she was one of them.

Although she was humiliated, beaten, stripped of all her defenses, lost, misled, yet she was pulled on by her own need to keep her head raised high, and by the certainty she shared with her mother that it was possible to create a life story quite different from that of the type of woman who had stayed at home taking care of the details in this room.

Now she had come to this parlor, something her mother should have done but had failed to do because she was so stubborn.

She heard a rooster crowing while the first rays of sunlight announced the dawning of a new day, even as the moon was still shining into the house. Along with the noise made by the cicadas and crickets, she could hear from deep within the house the sound of a lone guitar. Somebody was quietly strumming the strings, without passion or strength. There were some *zamba* rhythms but the song itself was no *zamba*, and some birds began to chirp in chorus as day was breaking.

Berta picked up her blue canvas bag and walked through the dark house that seemed so enormous, and whose uneven, shiny tile floors were as old as independence itself. She found her way to the patio where the *jacaranda* stood. Beyond it another wider patio opened up into the deepest recesses of the house, where she saw the silhouette of the huge mulberry tree that had sheltered its history. In its shade the old folks had rested in prayer and her grandfather had taken his naps with the red rooster, his "ally" as he called it, perched on his chest eating flies. That is where they still roasted meat, played cards, gambled, and decided who would get their votes at election time. They left only when something private had to be discussed, and it was the only place where men, family members or not, were allowed to cry when somebody had died and been laid out in the rooms opening on to the street.

The mulberry tree stood out imposingly against the early light, and at its feet sat an old man playing the guitar, ever so softly so as not to bother anyone. Berta, like some apparition attracted by the music, approached him and just stood there quietly, after saying "Good morning" in a whisper so low that it could hardly be heard.

Without looking up the old man said, "They came out today, look at them."

Although Berta could not see anything, she nodded as if she understood instead of questioning him. Then, still playing his peaceful melody, he showed her what he meant.

"There they are, and now they are here to stay because March is almost over: John the Evangelist and Magdalena."

Berta looked where he was pointing and saw two huge snails, extended to their full length, relaxed, and apparently quite comfortable on the ground that was wet with dew. Stretched out like a piece of gauze or tulle or a silk veil over a bride's head, they bravely spread out in all their soft strength, heads up, the four horns sticking out with an eye on each end, seeming to look at her and at each other.

"They don't like bright light, so they come out with the cool of the dawn or the evening and move around, but more than anything they like to come out right after a rain, and then they slither and scrape until the next year."

Was he playing the guitar for them? Were the snails listening? They looked majestic and moved along quite fast, stopping on the leaves to draw out the sap of the water in a sensual, clean embrace.

Berta and the man watched the march of the snails until they stopped in the folds of the mulberry tree. Seeing that, she realized that morning had arrived and that for the tree it was already fall, and the leaves were yellow, a yellow so bright that it was a life force, a yellow so beautiful that you just had to live to be able to describe it. She realized that she had never seen fall because in Tucumán it was always green and never changed, the never-ending work of the jungle. But here things came to a standstill because it was fall, and she was inside a house with an old man who played the guitar for two snails with holy names, and an aunt who looked like a toad and preserved the family history just as was done in any family. Except this time, Berta could and did say, "It is mine."

Then she decided to follow the snails' paths each dawn, and also the tracks left by a guitar's music. If she could have a religion, that is what it would be, and her stigmata, mark, would be her graying hair, a reminder of all she had lost, because of that balcony she would never look at again where they had thrown off her hopes and dreams. Yet, in spite of that, something from inside her was saying that there would be new roads to travel, though they might not be the same as the moist trail in the dew left by the two snails who, defying the season, had wanted to enjoy once more the sound of an old man's music.

10   Twenty-one Years Old

IT HASN'T BEEN EASY for me to understand, but I have finally realized that you just can't spend the rest of your life crying. Besides, in June I'll be twenty-one, when I can tell the world that I am a woman and when my mother can feel she has finished her work with me, that she brought me up and gave me her best. It's coming soon, and I'm wondering what will change, how much more will have happened between now and that day Mother has marked as some kind of fence or barrier I will have to climb over; a day that should have been happy because that was her plan, certainly happier than my fifteenth birthday that we couldn't celebrate because my father was dying. That birthday passed unnoticed, buried in all the vomit and fever, when his body weighed almost nothing, that feather my unlucky father had become, soon to be carried away by the wind. I was trying to help my mother find and give comfort, yet I knew that relief would come only with his death. So my party consisted of my father's death, when he "shut down," as the neighbors put it, and the relief that it was finally over.

Of course, that sense of relief caused me to feel like garbage. And garbage is my word for all the rosaries my mother was praying while constantly changing his sheets that he kept soiling in his agony. And it was garbage that my little brothers had to be left with the neighbors so they wouldn't see their father die and then cry at the wake where I was actually happy, because my papa would no longer have to suffer. I wanted him dead already. There was no way I could believe in any God that would treat anybody so shabbily, especially my father. He had not been a bad person, only a Peronist who had put his country first, followed by the "movement," next his buddies, then his wife, then my four brothers because they were males, and finally me.

My mother grieved without feeling sorry for herself, and she started to wear black even before he died and still does. My four brothers, devastated, cried until they choked, and their pain made me hate the dead man for dying and making his children suffer like that. We buried him without understanding everything we were burying with him; I felt so peaceful yet angry all at the same time. The neighbors whispered that I was stubborn as a mule, cold and selfish, that I was only concerned about being a good student and did not give two cents about anybody else. After all, a good daughter was supposed to cry, and if she didn't it could only mean that she hadn't really loved the one who died.

That day, when our living room was full of palms, his political buddies came, though it was a time when so many people were being forced into exile. My mother was praying non-stop beside the coffin, ignoring my brothers who needed her so badly. She was totally focused on that thing lying in the luxurious coffin they had gotten him, and on God, who had to be asked something a thousand times before he heard, or had to be threatened with his son's own mother before he would intervene with a miracle. My mother, who never tired of asking him for things, gave him all her attention instead of holding onto my brother Alberto and the twins, who were scared to death.

I was furious at her, with all her little religious images, and at the priests who made her feel guilty and afraid. I was sick of her dreams that told the future and then, when things did not turn out as she had predicted, the way she reinterpreted those same dreams with even more certainty; sick of her strength and acceptance of what she called "God's will," of her ignorance and refusal to recognize what science proved or history taught, and of the lousy education she had received and never complained about, one full of spirits, apparitions, and ghosts. What good had all that nonsense done her? It had only left her vulnerable enough to fall for the first guy who showed up and then got her pregnant, which is the same way so many other stupid people, such as her parents and siblings, had wasted their lives, even believing in "blessed are the poor." At that point, I really thought my mother was crazy, truly insane, though she managed to act like a normal person. Whenever anything bad or unfair happened to us, she closed off any discussion of it by uttering the word "mystery," which snuffed out any desire whatsoever that she might have had to discover the slightest bit of truth.

That same God who was the foundation of my mother's world had killed my papa in the prime of his life—I always wondered what he had done, how my papa could be any threat to the universe. He didn't mean anything anymore even in

Tucumán; he was only a bad word, because without Perón, when he got sick that was it—they reduced his hours and then finally fired him, robbing him of his meaning, good humor, and status in the community. He could no longer give out soccer balls or sewing machines sent by Eva; nobody cared about his suggestions or opinions, and his life had become one huge mistake from beginning to end because the poor, the *descamisados*, likewise had lost their "Conductor" and their "Saint." So now they had to put on a shirt or overalls or disappear to some faraway place because the Perón eras had ruined the country and my papa, who before had been a gentleman, was now a criminal. The best he could do was exactly what he did—get sick and die just as I turned fifteen.

Downstairs, at four in the morning after everybody else had gone home to sleep, his buddies were singing the "Peronist March" as they circled the coffin. My mother, still at the corpse's side and clutching her silver rosary, was lost in its painful mysteries and pleasures and didn't even hear the men. I just wanted to laugh at all of them for being such idiots, believing in unreal things and pure fantasies. Each of them had their own focus— my mother and her litanies, my papa's buddies singing, praising the guy everybody else was calling the biggest son of a bitch the country had ever known. They were singing as fervently as my mother was praying, and every single one of them was crying. Each one was grieving over huge losses, and the excuse was my papa, laid out there in the room, where it was hot, smelly, and full of flies that had to be swatted away. The heavens were getting ready to let loose a much-needed storm that would calm things down at least a little, but even the heavens were moving slowly that night.

I settled down to go to sleep in the armchair in the dining room where we were supposed to stay awake with him. I noticed the flower arrangement with the card, "Your wife and children." It was the one with the lilies, and it moved me because they were white and fresh and somehow expressed the best of my papa, the beauty he had had at one time. It was better to look at the lilies than at that monster coffin. It seemed to me that those flowers stood up straight and high in spite of everything, and that the hearse would take away my fifteen years, my mother's weeping, my father's suffering and Peronism, and everything about it that would never return to Argentina or to my life. The only thing left was a space, a scary one that I, with my maturing body, had no choice but to pass through.

▣ Tristán Nepomuceno

BERTA WAS DELIGHTED by the snails and their journeys, which unfolded as smoothly and gently as fall's colors. Her main focus was on gathering the dry leaves that collected in the patios and trying to predict how many more there would be the next day and the day after, and how long it would take for all the leaves to drop and for the coldest winds to arrive. She took it upon herself to burn the fallen leaves in the back where Tristán Nepomuceno would join her. Having retired from his various phases of public employment with its demands, he could now focus his energy on fixing broken-down objects in his shop at the edge of the property. There he had built his dwelling place and world with hundreds of red-painted cans full of all kinds of plants, the fruits of other people's generosity. The cans, set up in a certain order, wound in and out among the skeletons of old things waiting for him to restore them to life, like old pieces of furniture that the outdoor air was turning into good firewood because nobody thought to put a cover over them. That wait was part of the rhythm and logic that Tristán Nepo muceno applied to everything: just leave it lying around wait-ing to be fixed, suffering the effects of water, sun, and wind—a wind that brought earth-colored dirt and covered everything with a fine shade of years.

Berta had been hanging around him so much that she had gotten used to not talking to him because he, like all the Rieras, was a man whose silence was broken only occasionally by some monosyllable or melody from his guitar accompanied by his old voice which, though noticeably worn out, could still carry a tune. It was a soft and tired voice that did not expect to impress, seduce, or move anybody; it was directed inward, like everything about him. Berta sensed that her uncle was good for her, this man who was not her father or anybody else's, who had spent his life listening to and following orders, being diligent, ready and able to do as he was told or to serenade whomever his brothers chose.

He never did serenade his own girl, though, because within his bosom he had built an altar for his mother and dedicated his life to her, much to the dismay of his father who had always thought very little of him, even though he must have been handsome and gentle when young. Tristán Nepomuceno had failed to recognize his own manliness and good looks, stuck as he was in the midst of so many Riera men, so many strong machos while he was interested only in his mother. He had stayed in that house fixing furniture, faucets, and roof tiles that were always breaking because they had endured the earthquake of 1894, gales, and cat scratches, or simply spent hundreds of years covering the family. He fixed the peeling walls, the kerosene refrigerator, the gas stove, and his mother's iron—the electric iron he had bought for her with his first paycheck. He wanted her to stop going around with live coals that were dangerous for her as she concentrated on ironing out wrinkles and sprinkling starch on her husband's collars because that was woman's work and duty, at least a good woman's, as her grandmother used to say.

Tristán Nepomuceno had spent his life living in fear, afraid of blows that might never be struck, of teasing that he almost certainly did often get, of teachers and schoolmates, of soldiers and police, of bosses, neighbors, other guys, and his brothers. But mainly it was the fear of causing pain to his mother, that saint of all virtues, the woman in whom he saw angels and God and felt heaven opening up to touch her head, his mother who no other woman could ever measure up to, who told him that "nobody in the world loves the way a mother does," which must have been true if she said it. Because of all that, his fate was sealed in that child's love that from the very beginning he knew would bring him disappointment in everything that was not his mother. If some other woman did stir him, it was because her eyes or petite hands or feet or silence were like his mother's. But such a woman never knew of his interest, because he never got up the courage to stand before her and want her as she was, a real woman.

And that was the story of Tristán Nepomuceno's life: a good man through and through, good Christian, good relative, good neighbor, and good employee. A good guitar player, drinker, and cook, good even with the iron when his mother got sick, good with plants and the small mechanized gadgets that make up a home, good with the small herd of horses the family used to have, and even known to be good with the goats, which ate out of his hand no matter how skittish they usually were.

Berta felt that when she was with her Uncle Tristán Nepomuceno, she was always learning something, something she could not quite put her finger on but that gave her a little peace when she needed it, something that came through without words, for they did not talk while she was helping him with the dry leaves and the hundreds of plants in the red cans. This forest of flowers, furniture, old tires, chains of every thickness, various nuts and bolts, incredibly old tools for the most amazing purposes, and pieces of all kinds of things that just got older because of lack of use. Not to mention the empty cans, so many cans ready to become planters. The radio was usually on, the sound of it bringing in a murmur of the world that separated her uncle, old as he was, from the world.

12 Ave María

AUNT AVELINA HAD GIVEN Berta some hand-me-down clothes from an old chest so that she began wearing a robe and slippers. She had her long hair pulled back in a ponytail, the way she had worn it when little, and she even had on half socks like her aunt's. She swept the house, sometimes singing and sometimes silently. She mended clothes and sewed with her aunt before ironing and darning socks at *mate* time, which was long and not made for people to sip anything other than their own patience. On Tuesdays they made bread and tortillas, and on Fridays they put the beans to soak for Saturday, because that was when Uncle Tristán Javier came in from the country and gobbled up bean stew with lots of red sausage, his favorite meal.

He had been coming down every Saturday for more than twenty years to sell kid goats in the market and share the profit with his siblings, because those sales were the fruit of all the family possessions: thirty-five hundred hectares of rocky land where the goats scrambled over the same paths carved out by the first herds brought over by the Spaniards after the conquest. In four hundred years, the goats had not needed to change their location because the soil had turned out to be capable of supporting their awkward haughtiness and their quadruped instinct for scavenging the tiniest and most tender bites that such unfertile land could offer up, whose boundaries could be appreciated only in late afternoon, the hour when the color of everything was changing. In full daylight, everything the Rieras owned looked like nothing but gray earth but, with the low lights of sunset, it changed to a full scale of bright colors. Then the cane stalks in the desert would be blue, the hills red, the thick walls violet, and the gray would change to orange while dark greens would spread out over the vast expanse even as the sun was going down, until the bluish black La Rioja night covered everything once again leaving the land ready for dawn, the way it had been for centuries. In this land, time could not be measured in years but rather in eras: when it was an ocean bed, when it survived a cataclysm, when the earth dried up and the mountains formed, when forests grew and then caught fire and huge animals thrived before becoming extinct, and afterward, when everything became quiet and calm, like today, in that dried up land waiting for its own eternity, the rigid eternity one could read into the remaining cliff sculptures.

At lunch on Saturdays, which was at twelve sharp because her uncle got up early, the old ones always talked about the same things: the neighbors, the goats, kids of these goats, and those from way back who were no good for anything except for making people think up stories to tell and being called "unmannerly creatures." They also talked about the uncle's store in Olpa and the past—everything always told and retold in the same repeated phrases, always said in the same order, which served as a review of the family reminiscences that updated the inventory of stored memory about relatives, children, grandchildren, great-grandchildren, and their baptisms, deaths, and failures to marry, which were many. Weddings were few and far between in La Rioja.

On one of those days, when they were finishing up the after-lunch talk and Aunt Avelina was already choosing from her pile of graphic novels, ready to sit and read under the mulberry tree, Berta heard:

"Purest Ave María!"

"Conceived without sin!" answered Aunt Avelina, who quickly threw down what she had in her hand and exclaimed: "But if it isn't Miss Cholis, and here I was about to forget!"

And then a pale, thin woman in her early fifties came inside, her sharp high heels clicking through the patio, dressed in a fake Chanel suit, her dyed blonde hair long, with bangs, her heart-shaped lips colored passion red, and a small purse on her wrist. Miss Cholis had the voice of a young soprano and enormous blue eyes, all made up so they could be seen for miles, which lent her an expression of surprise that might have been permanent, eyes that were so beautiful they could be seen in the dark, like cat's eyes.

She was Aunt Avelina's friend, an expected visitor, and any men in the house knew to leave them alone because they talked women's talk. Miss Cholis was highly respected in La Rioja for her fine manners and impeccable look, that of an Argentine teacher, and indeed she was the most important music teacher in the most elite school, "Number One, José de San Martín," where she had taught both morning and afternoon sessions without a day's absence in seventeen years. Before that, she had graduated as Professor of Piano with highest merit and a medal from the Albeniz Conservatory, a private school with a national reputation.

"You were about to forget, *Negrita*!" Miss Cholis said to Aunt Avelina, with the same intonation as in "and now we will sing the 'Hymn to Sarmiento,'" while she strutted beneath the *jacaranda* tree in the patio as if she were parading down the catwalk in a beauty pageant.

"No way, Cholis! Gray hairs are unforgiving, and today is the fifteenth!"

They got together on the fifteenth of the month to dye each other's gray hairs, drink *mate* and fill each other in on all the gossip. Aunt Avelina would bring out the record player and they would take turns playing records. Miss Cholis would bring Chopin nocturnes played by Dinu Lipatti and Aunt Avelina would play Armando Manzanero and sometimes a *milonguita* by Tita Merello, who had been her spiritual guide ever since the graphic novels *Nocturne* and *Circular Saturdays*. If Aunt Avelina at some point had wished she had a different body, face, or voice, it was because of Tita Merello and wanting to sing *milongas* as a contralto, be a movie star, and smoke like Merello did, full of self-confidence, thrusting out her prominent bust in front of men.

While they dabbed each other with the goo for coloring their gray hairs, Miss Cholis would talk about her boyfriend, El Coco. She went on at length about Coco's many problems, and the money they were saving for their wedding day, which was always getting postponed so that now they had been "engaged" for sixteen years. It was just that things were always happening to Coco for he was such a good son, good brother, and good friend that he regularly had to help somebody out and thus had to work extremely hard as a traveling salesman, peddling stainless steel cookware and knives. Occasionally he sold jewelry—chains and earrings that he would sometimes give to Miss Cholis, because she was the love of his life and so that everybody would know that El Coco was the one who had given them to her—as he went round about in La Rioja and his life in a light green Rambler with reclining seats and automatic transmission.

Listening to the music from the record player, while the dye did its work on their heads covered with plastic caps and while they were wrapped in towels that reached to their waists, they would sit in the parlor, smoking the king size light cigarettes that Miss Cholis brought, as they both relaxed with their legs crossed like men, oblivious to how high their skirts might slide up, like the grown women they were, like women tired of putting up with everything. Tired of creating parties and meals, birthdays and birthday cakes, needlepoint tablecloths, curtains, and bedspreads woven out of scraps of multicolored wool; tired of decorating the window sills with flower pots and protecting them from the wind and hail; tired of buying little ceramic flower vases and plastic flowers to go on top of the television or the bureaus in the bedrooms; and tired of fantasizing the way women do in order to get through life, to live in the house they get, and to survive the illness and aging of their loved ones and also the ones they don't love but still have to put up with, their bosses and jobs and bills, and love that never turns out the way it does in novels. But at least it is love and that's what enables them to keep on going, with their furniture and children and daughters-in-law, or homes without children and daughters-in-law but with dogs and cats, or whatever they can get, even a turtle, roses and lilies, or whatever daisy springs up in their garden.

Berta listened to them talking in tones more serious than the ones they normally used in their roles as women in a world. With other people, they were always encouraging to live, eat, sing, believe in something, to learn the national anthem and the steps to the dance for the upcoming school presentation, to learn not to fight, to say "please" and "thank you" even if it was only part of the pledge of allegiance to the flag, or to get the old folks to look forward to somebody's next birthday, to the rainy season, or something, anything to give them a reason to keep living.

She watched the late afternoon come in through the window panes; the women did not turn on any lights because they were enjoying that faint darkness changing so quickly, knowing that once they turned on the lights, they would also set in motion all their duties and chores at the service of others, all those others they held up with their own small strength without anybody, including themselves, realizing it.

She studied them without being seen, in that moment of hair dyeing when they were speaking openly, in the deepest and clearest voice each one had. And she stayed right there next to the door until Miss Cholis saw her in the mirror and told her in her teacher's voice:

"Come near the hearth, my child."

13 Perhaps

FALL PASSED and the Southern Hemisphere winter arrived with a freezing, dust-laden wind that drove everybody inside by four in the afternoon while it whipped the clothes hanging on the line and threatened the delicate plants in cans. Uncle Tristán Nepomuceno settled even more into his little dwelling behind the house, taking with him as many of the plants as he could. They would spend the winter with him and share his fate "no matter what might happen," as he put it.

Aunt Avelina packed away the summer clothes and brought out the embroidered bed covers from Catamarca that decorated the beds with the buds of enormous, completely imaginary flowers that stood out against their dark background. They had been embroidered by hands that for generations now had been sleeping the sleep of the just. She also brought out the huge, heavy blankets that weren't really all that warm so everybody had to sleep in wool socks and thick clothing anyway. That was preferable to using those blankets of stiff, rustic wool that caused horrible nightmares when they touched the sleepers, who would feel completely alone, vulnerable, and naked as they faced the life and death situations all those dreams placed them in during the night.

Berta was sleeping in the room that had been Uncle Tristán Clímaco's, the uncle they hardly ever talked about, who lived with his wife in Buenos Aires and didn't keep in touch with the family very well. The room had been closed up for several decades before Aunt Avelina fixed it up for her.

Berta did the best she could to warm up the bed, which had been Grandmother Justina's until she died. The bed had been disassembled after Uncle Tristán Clímaco moved out, and the pieces stored in the saddle room with the fur saddle pads and the leg protectors, the same room where the spurs, crops, and lassos—given to each brother at birth by her grandparents—were still hanging on the wall, glinting in the dim light. All of that was from when the ranch still had good horses and Old Man Celestino Riera used to stay out in the countryside for months and even cross over into Chile with his cattle; when the grandmother was a woman with strong legs and statuesque arms, with enough energy for dancing so hard she left footprints on national holidays, and making five hundred empanadas in half a day. The Old Man even managed to keep that hard-working family, some cows, some crops, and some power, as well as plans for reaping something from that stony ground until he died and the grandmother hit hard luck and the children chose to work in the public sector rather than in the country. The railroad and governments sank the town even deeper into ruin, and the hot dry wind of La Rioja took care of the rest, so that the few with an enterprising spirit gave up, and people just kept leaving as they had for centuries.

In one way or another, most of the Rieras got out of there, each with a particular way of doing things, each trying to make it in the best way possible, to create a place to survive, have clothing, get help and television, and not be, under any circumstances, talked about by anybody who might be able to harm them or their property, here on earth as it would be in heaven. But their security was bound up in words they would not utter. They were people who did not talk any more than necessary. Such people would never in any context use the word "change," or the word "evolution" (by now linked to sin), or "atheist," "free thinker," "intellectual," "political," or the word "utopia," for example, because all of those words might create the impression that one was a revolutionary. But the two most important words that should never be said were the worst: the most dangerous one, "sex," was already the most disastrous of all words; and "love" was a word to be careful about for it was okay when said by women but really bad when used by men except in the context of Christ and his church.

The Rieras who stayed in La Rioja learned well how to survive and had nothing to hide, because they did absolutely nothing that could not be done with the door to the house unlocked day and night, as it had always been. They did good and charitable works as much as possible, kept each other company throughout life, and prepared each other and themselves for death. They took care of their possessions and of themselves, not bothering anybody or being bothered, and according to the occasion, playing the guitar, celebrating San Nicolás and the Virgin, and kneeling three times before the Child Jesus on December 31. They gave the goats the most outrageous names;

used traditional remedies and comforts and ate broth when they suffered colds and discomfort; swept the walk in front of the house and took care of the parlor furniture; and were sufficiently amazed every time Uncle Nepomuceno's snails returned right on time every spring, to come up with some words about the journey of life and the return of all those things that give and support life, while in the middle of those cycles continuing to put away the embroidered blankets when the warm weather arrived, asking for and giving blessings in the time of blessings, and beating their chests during Lent.

Berta, who had heard her mother criticize them, watched them, understood their work, their feelings, and more than anything, the importance of their fears, because they had already gone through the misfortunes currently facing Berta, and now, lying there in the bed, wrapped in the heavy Catamarcan blanket, she said to herself: "Perhaps, just maybe, this is what life is all about."

Viditay, ya me voy
y se me hace que no he'i volver
malhaya mi suerte tanto quererte
vidita, y tenerte que perder
malhaya mi suerte tanto quererte,
viene clareando mi padecer.

Darling of my life, I am leaving
Never to return.
Loving you so much,
Life of mine, and having to lose you
Is my bad luck, loving you so much,
My suffering is clearly dawning.

04 The Messenger

WHEN I SAW THE MAN known to everybody in Villa 9 de Julio as Mr. ThousandFive, I saw my house, my mother and brothers, and I think, even Atilio alive, my books on the kitchen table, and my mother's knitting next to the pot of freshly brewed hot coffee. "So that my daughter won't poison herself with artificial things," she always said.

The purpose of the coffee she made for me, like everything else, was to prepare me and help me fulfill the dream, my own dream and my mother's dream, the one that according to her, all my female relatives—even my great grandmothers—had had. I would be a physician! This daughter would be important, would not have to depend on a man or anybody else, and would prove that it was possible to overcome all kinds of misfortune—her father's death, their lack of income, inheritance, or important family name. She would do all this through sheer willpower and study.

I saw Villa 9 de Julio's smokestack, the slaughterhouse lit up from three in the morning, my Mercedes Sosa records, my guitar sheet music, my mother's black frying pan that was always sticking so that she daily threatened to throw it out and buy another. The day she actually did that, though, had never arrived, like so many others filled with promises she regularly made. I saw my book of stories, the one my father bought for me, with the tale about the stork that got mixed up and delivered the wolf pup to the sheep and the lamb to the wolves, and how each group loved their own baby and refused to exchange them when the nearsighted old stork tried to correct its error. I saw the neighbors at siesta time drinking *mate* underneath their rubber plant, that sweetest and most delicious *mate*, because they always added honey and pennyroyal, cedar, mint, and fresh grass that my childhood friend Sylvia prepared. I saw the church where my mother goes to the seven o'clock mass and cooks for people even more poor than we are, and where at the entrance is the only white oak tree I have ever seen, and where dogs are admitted for the mass dedicated to San Roque. I saw the street that becomes a thick mud hole after the hot, crashing rains. I saw my school and the caper spurge that grows beside the railway tracks and gives shade to a cross that marks where the train ran over a young boy, and to his mother who goes up there every afternoon out of her mind with guilt, because she hears the child calling her but cannot reach him before the train swallows him up. And, finally, I saw the photo of my graduation, my dreams and hopes set on getting ahead, and my mother holding in her hands the family treasure, my bachelor's degree.

But here in front of me was Mr. ThousandFive, dressed in his Sunday best that my mother made him wear when he went to church. Somebody had given him a dead man's suit so my mother wouldn't scold him for being scruffy. I immediately knew what was up even before he greeted me with the words:

"Berta, your mother sent me."

It was his whole appearance, the way he could not meet my gaze, his voice lower than before, his eyes redder and more watery, looking at the floor stones, that convinced me that nothing would ever be the same, that Tucumán would never again be some republic's garden, and that my city, my neighborhood, the Villa, could no longer be called mine. All that was finished, like an era or age that comes to an abrupt halt. The road back was closed to me, I had lost everything that used to be mine, and I was no longer there and never would be. But the worst part was that at the same time I knew I could never erase that place from my heart and mind. I was and always would be a child from Villa, and my mother would always be a full-fledged Matadero woman. But I had been thrown out, like Atilio off the balcony, into a future facing nowhere—or everywhere in the world except Matadero in Villa 9 de Julio.

"You must be tired, Mr. ThousandFive," I said to him.

"A guy who works with the cold storage brought me in his truck, and after his delivery I'm going back with him this afternoon."

He gave me a packet wrapped up in brown paper with string tied around it for added security, like a package of meat. Then he took an envelope out of his undershirt and I saw my mother's handwriting. Mr. ThousandFive had recently shaved, most likely in response to one of my mother's suggestions, and I noticed that he had a little bread with him. He was wearing loafers that didn't look right on him, as he was a man of sandals and overalls.

For many years, Mr. ThousandFive had been a meat cutter in Matadero, as well as a street vendor hawking entrails and offal that he sneaked out and offered for sale in the neighborhood. He took this around in a cart he had created from the shell of an old refrigerator by adding two wheels and handlebars. He shared the business with his brother, Rococo, who was quite black, as opposed to Mr. ThousandFive who was white, with very light blue eyes and skin reddened by too much heat or cold. They were both somewhere between sixty and seventy years old and lived in a tin and cardboard shack next to the bakery in a wasteland belonging to who knows who. Clearly they were not full brothers, but in the Villa that did not matter because a mother makes all her children siblings whoever the father might be. What matters is the pot from which they eat and the roof to which they come home together. They passed through the neighborhood at mid-morning, completely silent, with their vehicle full of hearts, livers, and stomachs, never shouting their product "out of respect for the poli" since their business was not legal. But they also never failed to leave a few kidneys at the nearest police station to keep the captain happy. When city inspectors showed up in the neighborhood, the two brothers simply closed the top of the refrigerator so that it looked as if they were just moving it.

The neighborhood gossip had it that in a matter of minutes Mr. ThousandFive could carve up a cow with the precision of a surgeon, and that for years he had had a horse for sale for the exorbitant price of 1,500 pesos, possibly because he didn't really want to part with the animal. That is how he got his nickname "ThousandFive;" nobody knew any more what his real name was, nor that of his brother Rococo. There was also a story that there had been a woman who had cheated on him with another man, an infamous Chileno, and that Mr. ThousandFive had wounded him in the arm in a duel. The wounded man had disappeared without ever reporting the matter to the police, because he, the loser, was as macho as Mr. Thousand-Five. After that, Mr. ThousandFive dedicated himself to drinking, along with his brother.

At some point, my mother took him on as a project. Whenever Mr. ThousandFive failed to show up on the streets, she would dispatch one of my brothers to the shack to see if he was alive. If he couldn't get up, she would send him a plate of food; then, when he had recovered, he would help my mother with some household chore, such as picking up the garbage or simply serving as a watch dog, because in my house there were no men, only my mother, me, and the boys. Later, when Mr. ThousandFive quit drinking for good—something my mother called a miracle of the Sacred Heart of Jesus—he started hanging out with her every evening, watching soap operas. There he would be, sitting on the sofa with my mother, who would always be knitting, and he would cry like a baby when sad things happened on television. Both of them made sure I did not get distracted from my lessons, though; they never let anybody make a noise until I finished studying.

Now here he was, bringing me a package and a letter from my past, and I would have hugged him if it hadn't seemed somewhat inappropriate, for he was a vagabond and I a young girl overwhelmed by all I had lost; that afternoon, though, he seemed like a father.

San Miguel, Tucumán, June 10, 1976

Dear Daughter,

Mr. ThousandFive will take this letter to you, and I hope it finds you in good company with my brother and sister. Let him know how you are doing and give my regards to all my family.

I pray for you, dear, to Our Lady of the Helpless, from Sevilla, and to San Nicolás of Bari, for it lifts my heavy heart. I hope that you are praying too and that your life will get straightened out.

Happy birthday, my child. You have reached adulthood, and I give thanks to God for every day you and I keep living, and I pray for wisdom to survive in these extremely difficult times. Mr. ThousandFive is bringing this letter to you because it is not a good idea to send it through the mail; at least, this heart of a mother is telling me it would be dangerous. There is a lot of activity here every night and sometimes during the day, with people being taken away, especially young people and students, but even some whole families.

People are leaving Tucumán: the Canadian priests at the Church of Consolation have returned to their country, for they have been expelled and

would be in danger here, and Father Víctor came to
bid me good-bye and to tell me that you must not
come back until this all clears up. He left me his
Latin Bible, saying I should not show up at church
with the Spanish version of the Bible because it
is considered dangerous.[10] So, Daughter, I burned
it, may Our Lord forgive me, just as I burned your
boyfriend's books and all those papers he left in
the house, and I burned your photographs and his
and those of your classmates as well, because when
they go into houses they look for photographs,
and address books, and books on politics. They
have outlawed Jehovah's Witnesses, so those people
think they must flee for they are now considered
criminals simply because they refuse to salute
and swear on the flag or participate in military
service. That is why the Anachuris family just do
not know what they are going to do. The Ramírez
family, who own the bakery next to where Mr.
ThousandFive lives, have had their home entered
and all the sons were taken. The ones who did it
told Mr. Ramírez not to look for them because if
he did they would come back and take him as well.
When people are taken away, they never return, but
they don't show up dead either or in the hospital.
Nobody knows anything and people's neighbors just
aren't talking at all. On top of everything,
they say they are going to close the Matadero
factory for good, because they say it is full of

politicians and unionists. They say they will just vacate it and set up a police station in the neighborhood.

Don't worry about us as your brothers are fine and I am too. But do not come back or even call or write to us. Don't talk to anybody you don't know and trust. Be courteous with your aunt and uncles and appreciate the hand that feeds you. Even if only for this one time, you must be humble and obedient.

Nobody ever comes to the house any more, and the truth is that I never visit any of the neighbors either. Ever since you left and with all that has happened, I try not to talk to anybody and nobody talks to me or stops in to ask about you. I know they are talking about you but nobody approaches me to say anything. I am alone with only your brothers. The one person who does come to see me every day, and without asking any questions, is Mr. ThousandFive. He is more helpful than ever and is much better, as you know, now that he no longer drinks. Still, sometimes he gets sick because of high blood pressure but he doesn't dare go to the clinic for fear of being taken to the hospital or the police station where they would find something, anything, suspicious about him and take him away like the others. I make sure he is never without food and he in turn runs errands for me and helps with heavy things around the house. He is going to take this letter to you, along with these little things I am sending. You can trust him and should tell him how you are. Please take good care of yourself, my child, for one day you will be a mother yourself and will know what it feels like, and that we are here to suffer just like our Mother Mary. In spite of it all, though, our greatest gift and mission in life is being a mother, because that is how we do our part in our Lord's work.

This is a vale of tears, and the best we can do is live virtuous lives as good people. There are many ways to live, but always remember that no matter what might happen, the best way is to be a good and honorable woman. Please know that I carry my head high because of you and your deceased father.

May your twenty-first birthday find you in good health. You are old and wise enough to be your own best guide.

Give my regards to my sister and brothers, and for you I send a mother's blessing.

Amalia del Valle

15 Hell

AUNT AVELINA had looked at Mr. ThousandFive in her toadish way, ready for the attack, ready to spit straight into the horrible messenger's eye. It infuriated her that a man so disreputable-looking and of such low social rank, who was dirty even when clean, could use her sister's name and dare to converse with her niece, who by now everybody in the neighborhood knew was such a proper young woman. Berta had come to be with her and Uncle Tristán Nepomuceno because they were old and needed care; she was simply doing as her mother, Avelina's fine widowed sister in Tucumán, had so thoughtfully asked her to do.

Aunt Avelina was a confident author, and upon seeing her niece she had been able to imagine the plot for "Berta's soap opera." There had been no need to ask Berta any questions when she arrived because her story was of course no different from those in the graphic novels, printed in greenish gray on fully illustrated pages that the aunt was constantly reading. It might go like this:

A beautiful young woman, inexperienced and naïve, flees a romance that did not work out and takes refuge with her austere family in La Rioja, where she is able to recover her balance that was never really lost, because there is no doubt about her virginity. She has the heart of an innocent child and thus turns to her aunt, for it is like being in the arms of her own mother. Her aunt will guide her down the paths of religion and good sense and keep her safe until that day when "he" will surely arrive, the knight in shining armor, of course, with his entourage of angels and violins, riding on a white horse if possible. They will prepare flowers and her wedding veils: one to be kept in the aunt's glass cabinet and the other for the Virgin, according to custom. And life will go on because that is the purpose of a woman, to have a family and an aunt such as this one, who asks no questions because it is obvious that what is hidden in the heart of a young woman who cries through the night are love's secrets.

Berta let her go on believing this novel that she had sketched out in her mind, for it did not seem possible to tell her the other story that in no way fit her aunt's familiar grand myth. Immersed in her graphic novels, her aunt was an authority on happy endings that allowed for evil only so far as "every cloud has its silver lining." That is how she nurtured her spirit with what she was lacking and had never had or had lost for good. The best part about these graphic novels is that they needed very few words; words often just complicated things. In them a young girl was a virgin, and a good man always respectable; a religious woman, a saint; lawyers, all bad; but doctors, good. Characters always claimed their rightful inheritance and true identities were revealed. And then finally, at the very end, heroes and heroines were reunited amidst copious tears of emotion, love, and hope. The life of Berta's aunt consisted of a wide variety of boleros and tears, and the novels she fantasized out of her everyday world served as a screen to hide any plots that did not conform to these. That way, through the precious moments of her reading, true stories could be turned into something that helped her survive, because of the hope and expectation for never-ending hugs and happiness shared forever, sealed with engagement rings that would never lose their connecting power. Armed with that predictable paper world, in two colors only, easily accessible with pages that could so effortlessly be turned during siesta time, one certainly could go on smiling at life, face misfortune as if it did not exist, and see that everything makes sense. Even Berta's current situation, which in reality made no sense whatsoever, could be forced into the same framework.

Because of all this Berta understood why her aunt retreated angrily into the house with an expression of disgust at seeing her treat Mr. ThousandFive like an old friend. Before leaving, she made it quite clear that the man should not be invited inside; indeed, she seemed to think he would do well to disappear, given that he was not a character worthy of appearing in any of her book panels or being a protagonist in any plot.

"Hmmm. . . . My sister Amalia certainly has stooped low, depending on people like this! I hope none of the neighbors sees him!" grumbled her aunt as she left.

Berta did not want to cross her and so stayed in the doorway with Mr. ThousandFive. He told her he was going with his traveling companion to the market where they would eat, and then they would return home. Lowering his voice as much as possible, he told her:

"Tucumán is hell, worse than before. Don't go back there. Instead, get far, far away. Your mother doesn't know all that I know. They are looking for you, on the heels of Atilio; they don't know who you are, but they are looking for you. They don't even know your name, but when they find out that you were Atilio's woman, they will seize you and everybody connected to you. Apparently, they are looking for money they believe Atilio had in the headquarters of the Tucumán Federation of Sugar Cane Workers. I am talking about the hooded guys— they seem convinced that there is a woman, Atilio's sweetheart, who kept the money he must have had, and that's why they have raided the homes of Atilio's associates, looking for you, and trying to make people tell them the name of his woman."

Berta stood frozen to the spot. She felt all kinds of things at once: the possibility of death; the cold of the anatomy room; the trembling the first time she was naked facing her lover; the horror of others' torture that now felt like her own; disgust, powerlessness, humiliation; the worst fear you could possibly feel, the fear of falling from a building of a thousand floors, knowing during the fall that this was just the antechamber of the most horrendous death—her own and that of her people. She felt guilty, a most intense shame for having believed in those absurd words of political hopes, that now nobody even dared utter, and for having stepped out of the expected story and committed herself to that man without the rings that are supposed to bind a man and woman together, indeed without anything more than a look—that man whose sole purpose in life was to make sure their country was not part of a graphic novel, but rather a place in the real world. His land would be one where Mr. ThousandFive and his traveling companion could play a role, even if it was not a lead role; where they could at least be members of the cast so that at the end of the show they would have the honor of seeing their names appear in the list of actors; where she could embrace a man like him without creating problems, where it would be okay.

And because she had believed in all that and had loved unconditionally the man who fully believed in such a dream, she was now trash, a woman who was compromising everybody who wanted to help her. Unfortunate as she herself was, she was also killing her mother and destroying her brothers because of what a disaster she was, just because she had allowed herself to get involved after hearing Atilio talk as she sat on the sidewalk. She caused so much trouble by loving him and loving everything he was saying. He was describing to the crowd a world where you could actually manage to be alive. She had been foolish to tell her mother about all those ideas; her mother had responded that the family had already suffered enough with Peronism and now, oh, no, not my daughter too! She had been a fool to give herself to that man who had nothing to offer her and no real way to help her. She had given everything possible to Atilio, who now, as always, was way ahead of her because he was dead and thus would not have to pass through hell—the hell he had left her in and, of all things, without him.

Berta managed to stay calm, for clearly the thing to do was to keep her mouth shut about how she was feeling. Besides, she was afraid of what else she might hear.

"Thank you, Mr. ThousandFive. Please tell my mother that I'm fine."

That was all, everything else had become a knot that began in her throat and extended all the way to her stomach. She went into her room and curled up in Grandmother Justina's bed, trying to surround herself with its many years of stability and good sense, until the night hid the truth that anybody could have read on her face.

1⑥ The Window

SHE STAYED IN THAT ROOM for three days and three nights, going through all kinds of torment that she supposed would prepare her for when she herself would have to face the all-too-real torture that her friends, neighbors, and colleagues were surely already suffering. She thought about people in Tucumán, just regular people like her, being dragged by their hair, locked up in car trunks, hands tied behind their backs. She could hear their screams as well as the ones of others now silenced. She cried at the kicks, the thousands and millions of kicks that others must be receiving, she saw their bruises, their sores and stripped fingernails, and their swollen mouths so deformed that they would never again be able to express anything. And the teeth falling out like petals on the air, their eyes bulging out of their sockets, and a shoe, stray, without its mate, lying near the entrance of a house, where the light would stay on forever because a family would be endlessly searching for somebody.

She suffered through those three nights lying on the floor on the old Catamarca quilt with embroidered flowers. Somehow the earth beneath the floor gave her the support she needed to face the nightmares whose actors never had hands, much less fists, to close up tight and use as a defense. They were all blaming her, while she waited for her cursed hour to arrive, in that darkness that was the sum of all her panic. All the horror fit into the insignificant rectangle of a pillow soaked by the silent tears of a young woman. She smothered her terror in the pillow, and this was about as far as her freedom reached. That was all the freedom she and her people had. People who, though she did not yet know it, would stand together in solidarity because of the lamps being lit suddenly in the night, or the quick unexpected movements inside a house, or the low voices over the phone asking for or giving information about the most horrible things. It always happened at that hour of the day when dawn is just barely breaking, making the helpless even more powerless and even more alone, the people who have nowhere to turn in their search for information about their loved ones snatched from them.

But the sun still rose each day to spread its light, clearing out the noises—and the silence as well—of the night that kept reminding her of the final outcome: the car that would stop in front of the house; the hooded men who would come in to take her away; the weapons, the commands, and the terror of her aunt and uncle who would defend themselves and try in vain to protect her. She was already prepared to remain silent and withstand the pain to her body and the tearing of her soul; to put up with it until everything would go to hell, or insanity would set in so she could just say all right, enough already. Or who knows? Maybe she would tell them what they wanted to hear, even if she didn't know anything, inventing any old plot and finally singing in her own holocaust like Santa Cecilia, the patron saint of music, so she could pass quickly through the corridor of death and turn off the light. Because that must be what death is, just a light switched off and that's it, with nothing left for those who remain except the silence of the person who will never say another word.

It had happened to Atilio and his brother Mauro, and who knows how many others before, throughout all the conflicts of this human race, to which she soon would no longer belong. In her nightmare she kept asking herself angrily where that angel could be, her own, the one each person was supposed to have according to her mother. Where in the world was God on all those nights of kidnapping and martyrdom, bullets, and blood; of separating children from their parents, spouses from spouses, brothers, sisters, and friends from each other? Where could God possibly be, a God who let loose this angel that would appear at the worst moments of sleeplessness, so happy that people were nothing but idiots whose heads were empty except for graphic novels.

And then the angel appeared to her, right in front of her, laughing at her in loud cackles, telling her, Atilio, and Mauro that it was already too late, that they had missed the train—the train of history they mentioned over and over—and thrown their youth and beauty, health, intelligence, and good sense to the dogs. The damned angel, the same one that had deceived her poor mother, was nothing more than pure evil. The angel was going around all over the miserable republic, shining his light on the executioners, making them believe that they, too, were acting in his name and representing him, which was the same as working for God and his Christian civilization. Yes, it was the same angel that made fun of Berta and her stupid family; and of the naïve ideas of Atilio and Mauro, those idealistic, foolish failures; and of their colleagues; and of Perón and Evita and Che and even Belgrano and San Martín.[11] Indeed, he made fun of everybody who had fallen into the trap of believing in the existence of the kind and good angel, the one that would make history march toward equality, science, and progress. The angel wore the face of the people and was the same one who had convinced Atilio of what he kept repeating to her: "The time has come for the liberation of the people; this is the day of the birth of the new society, the new person. It is the moment to leave everything behind that does not help fulfill this hour. Our personal lives will come later, after the tides of history, which can't be held back, have swept in this new society. Those of us who have accepted the role of leaders, the forward-looking ones, will resume our personal lives and goals later. You must wait for me, for right now I have to fulfill my commitment to my people."

"Shit-face angel," sobbed Berta.

She fasted except for liquids with bitterness and resignation, took stock of her life, and berated herself for not having had enough sense to pay attention to her mother, who kept telling her: "The poor have always been with us." And for believing— yes, she too—that life or history made sense.

The fever that took hold of her during those three days and nights brought her to the lowest ebb, making her vomit up the soups and herbal teas that her aunt gave her. She dreamed of Atilio, death, the angel, Tucumán caving in with an earthquake of explosions, sunk in the final judgment of souls in pain—young ones asking for help, calling for their mothers or fathers—that were flying around, horribly distressed, in circles above it all. It was Tucumán in red and black, burning, an oven, a slaughterhouse, a rotting sugarcane heap of people burning and angels were fanning the flames, and even the ones not in the flames were on fire. And a huge abyss was opening up and swallowing everybody, the ones already burning in the fires as well as those who thought they were safe—including herself, who was fleeing but barely keeping ahead because the angel was always there waiting for her at every rest stop along the road.

On the fourth day the fever and hallucinations ended. She could hear Uncle Tristán Nepomuceno bringing into the house what sounded like a piece of heavy metal, possibly furniture, probably something that somebody had thrown out and that he would put on the long list of things waiting to be repaired. Her aunt was frying onions, rice, and potatoes, filling the rooms with the smell of oil and vegetables, the familiar smell of home. It was a smell that said keep moving, life does not stand still and the world is still moving on, because evidently the sun was still making its way through the shutters over the windows, windows that had witnessed the last Indian attack, the May Revolution, the end of slavery, the rough *caudillos* of La Rioja, and the birth of a nation.

So much had happened outside that window that was flooding Berta with clarity. What she and her generation were suffering through could be catalogued as just one more frame in the long film, a brief moment in at least three hundred years of her ancestral home. And way back there stood the mulberry tree, straight and firm despite all the governments and unfortunate marriages and days of crying and mourning for the dead. There was that tree, naked, standing up to winter. Berta smiled because she still had a mouth, teeth, and tongue for smiling, and two eyes in her face, and two arms with fists, and five fingers on each hand, and she even still had calluses from playing the guitar, and ears to hear the hundreds of birds singing in front of that double-paned window. She smiled because she knew the secret of Uncle Tristán Nepomuceno's contented snails, which would now be hibernating, calm and hidden, waiting for good weather.

She got up, touching her face, chest, and legs, for it was true, yes, she was healthy and awake, and she had beaten the death hunters by at least three days.

Her aunt was waiting for her in the kitchen, making that noise with the pots that kept the appetite and stomach on a schedule, because life is what scares death; and it was written, according to her, by a graphic novel author, that good girls always have good lives—even better, good marriages. Everything was arranged in Avelina's mind: Berta would go to Olpa to forget the man who had made her cry so feverishly for three days and nights, to help her uncle Tristán Javier who had had kidney problems ever since he fell off his mare, and who needed help with the store and the sale of gasoline. He needed a pair of young arms to take care of the livestock and Divine Providence was sending this girl, so Avelina announced to Berta that she would be leaving for Olpa and there she would be distracted, in an environment so healthy that she would recover from the heartbreak of that love that had ended unhappily.

Berta believed that she might be safe there, at least until this sick winter was over and her country returned to its senses. So she agreed and left that very afternoon to allow life to bring some good things her way until the snails would awaken. It was a question of jumping toward the light in the window, a gift, to take and live one day at a time.

June 14, 1976

Dear Trini,

Some day maybe you'll read this letter because I'll have figured out how to get it to you. I know it won't be easy, as I don't even know where you're living now, but I feel the need to write down the things I remember most about you. And we always did find a way of getting our messages to each other, didn't we, and of talking during class despite the fact that our teachers didn't allow it, especially in math. I think often of the coded alphabet we invented, written in geometric shapes, points, lines, and arrows, that we used to write each other notes. We always managed to tell each other about the boys we liked.

Our school was the gem of the Universidad Nacional de Tucumán, remember how they called it the "breeding ground"? Out of that school would come the best professionals and managers, women capable of bringing to fruition everything the generation of 1880 had created. We took the big exam—it was really hard, wasn't it?—and we tied, you and I, for twentieth place, and we left crying because we thought we hadn't made it, but in the end we both did, you in history and me in biology.

Later, I got to go to your house and see your
grandfather's sculptures, "the huge bone heads"
as you called them, without showing much interest
in his great fame as an artist or the illustrious
lineage of your ancestors, despite the fact that
we studied in that dining room with princely
furniture. Even so, just like at my house, you all
carefully measured the size of the slices of bread
you cut to be sure there would be enough to go
around. As for our last names, neither of us could
complain, but that was it. At school we were known
as "the united dark girls" because we were always
together and everybody believed we were Peronists,
though we weren't.

You need to know what has happened, Trini. I
had to run away. You have no idea how far I am
from Tucumán, my house, everything. I miss you
and would oh so much love to be able to tell you
everything I am feeling, even if it had to be in
code, using our own alphabet. Now I understand
many of the things you used to say, in the
talks we had, and the fights you had at school
with the other girls and with your grandfather.
I understand now why you would lecture me for
being such a nitwit who refused to accept any
responsibility for our social reality, why you had
to fight those governments that just sucked up to
what you called the oligarchy, and their armies

that ever since Rosas never did anything except cover their own asses. I understand why you got so frustrated with me and would mutter under your breath that I was *pequebú*, a petit bourgeois, because you wanted me to join you but I didn't dare even consider the possibility of leaving my mother with the boys to dedicate myself to change and revolution. But look, all you predicted has happened and here I am unable to study, abandoning my mother and brothers after all, totally without Atilio, or any clue as to where all this endless repression is taking us.

I miss our walks, those all-nighters we spent strolling through Tucumán with Atilio and Pepe, the four of us, because Tucumán was alive at all hours, while you and they talked about Perón, Evita, Che. I miss the nights I spent with you, you knitting because your baby was on the way and you poking my leg while I drank coffee because I had to study all night for some test or assignment due the next day. I miss all of that—sharing every big decision of our lives, your marriage, med school for me, the birth of each of your babies, and helping you choose their names. Trini, if you only knew—now I am going away to live in the country, to a place called Olpa, where I am one of the oligarchy, a *"garca,"* because my mother still has some land—imagine that, *"garcas"* strapped with hunger. So maybe one of these days, when this unreal absurdity is over, you will come and together we will make a revolution, I don't know what, just some sort of revolution, though one certainly smaller than what you and your friends were planning.

I understand now, Trini, and I want you to know this despite all the time that has passed without our being in touch, why you left school and chose a life of so much sacrifice. I understand that, Trini, and I admire you and want to tell you that you are so brave, you're always way out ahead, you and your artisans, you and the people of the valleys, and your women weavers and potters, you talking to them about their rights, convincing them that they are capable, helping them conquer their fears, showing them all of that through their own art. You and your two beautiful sons, and that crazy Pepe—how could I not love you all, Trini? I miss you. I am in no position right now to judge whether what you were planning is good or bad or whether your ideas about making a country where women have dignity, workers have basic rights in their jobs, and all children have toys, are realistic. I don't know, Trini, whether you all are right or just completely crazy, but I do know that you always put your whole self into whatever you do because of your social conscience, your life and soul and everything, and that is why I am your friend. Atilio said it could be done with Perón; you said without him; Atilio said it was just a matter of reforming the military; you said that there had to be another army, one made up of the people. But for me, Trini—good daughter that I am of these people, of my mother, good student, good doctor—for me, my belief in the incredible marvelous human body has lit up every day of my life since we were students in high school, and I have left to you all those issues of social justice and history because I just don't have the head for all that, for mine is about healing, taking care of, and preserving life in my own way.

What you were right about, like Atilio, is all this repression that is happening. You said this would happen and few people understood. But you said it was time to speed up the struggle with more activity to create popular understanding and involvement and that the people would follow. Atilio said it was time to stop the protest actions and support the government until we could elect a new one, one that would be a people's government. You also said it had to be for the people, and I, who am one of the people and on the side of both of you, now don't have either of you.

I don't know where you are, if you are

in the mountains or some city, but I do know
that wherever you are, you are standing up for
everybody, including this *pequebú,* who is farther
away than you could imagine, not so much because
of miles as because of having left everything that
was my life. And you know what, Trini? I need you
so I can remember how to get myself back because
I know you would be able to draw me a map with
special markings just for me.

I am going to Olpa.

Berta

🔢 Olpa

OLPA WAS BEYOND Olta but before Olma, and on the few maps that actually showed it, it was merely a dot in the middle of a cross, the point where two roads intersected, where the traveler could tempt fate by selecting among the four cardinal directions. Anybody able to read a map knows that at whatever point you find yourself, there are always at least four ways out and maybe that is why nobody stayed in Olpa. Because it was a sparsely populated spot of sand and stone that, if seen from a distance, had the appearance of a lunar landscape. Still, once you got off the bus, you could see it had plenty of goats and a variety of thriving bushes—white *quebracho* trees and a few mesquite, so appreciated by the old-timers. Among the few signs of what might be called civilization still apparent long after the so-called civilizers had all but exterminated the Diaguita Indians, the most important was an old general store with a tin sign on the front that prayed, OLPA'S PROGRESS. Painted green and yellow over a white background on a sheet of metal now all rusty, with its top left corner bent at forty-five degrees, it swung to and fro in the wind. Instead of completely flying away, it simply accompanied the sound of the wind currents like an orchestra made up of old people already departed to other worlds, who still held on to a place here in order to enjoy making a little noise center stage late in the afternoon.

Olpa also had about five olive trees, slight traces of old vineyards and broad pepper trees, and a few houses covered with creeping vines of red and orange flowers and some paradise trees lining the land that was supposed to have been a plaza someday, affirming its vocation as a city. The narrow Church of Santa Rosa de Lima, patron saint of America, presided over all that plus the carefully kept cemetery set off from the houses, where once and for all so many of the Rieras were resting in peace, next to the Brizuelas, Sotomayors, Tellos, a few Ontiveros, Romeros, and here and there a gringo who had succumbed to the drought in these parts or simply not managed to put one foot in front of the other to make it through one of the four exits. Everything else was just as it had been on the seventh day when God rested. It was one vast expanse of pure nature where these descendents of the first Spaniards had settled early in the seventeenth century, thanks to a royal grant. The dust storms stirred up by the wind in the late afternoon marked the only change in a world that seemed completely calm and motionless. And though it hardly ever rained, even during the rainy season, the rains came in cyclical catastrophes that caused the amazing ravines carved out by nature, which were normally dry ditches, to overflow. Every now and then, there was a real flood that carried away shacks and animals.

Olpa retained its original Indian name. Being so small, inhospitable, and distant from any possible ambition, it apparently had not deserved to be rededicated, or even to have been officially founded in the first place. That act would have required more than the Church; it needed the presence of holy water and the cross on a sword, which might have rescued Olpa from its pagan state of original sin. Besides, it was stuck among numerous villages with even more impossible names that did not show up on maps: "Loneliness," "Envy," "Benediction," "Resistance," "Marvel," and "Smart One." Others went by names given to try to Christianize them: "San Nicolás de Bari," "Santa Josefa," "Santa Clara," "San Javier," "San José," "San Cristóbal," "San Francisco," "Santa Rita," and "San Pedro." And finally, there were the ones with family names whose lineage made it perfectly clear that this was no longer land belonging to the Incas, and much less to the Calchaquis or Diaguitas: "The Vegas," "The Alanices," "The Aguirres," "The Baldecitos," "Cordobes Well," "Lujann Mountain," and "Quinteros Mountain." And this world surrounding Olpa was right in the middle of the salt pits, "Ancient" and "Huge," which imposed their sterile majesty over everything.

As it did on La Rioja's plains, time here passed slowly and life could be organized however one might wish. This was especially true for those no longer in that stage called youth, when biology or just plain natural anxiety caused such a strong sense of haste. Everybody in Olpa who had felt a lack of whatever kind had already left. Most came back only briefly to share some sorrow and then never returned again. Others were just passing through. That is why Uncle Tristán Javier would get up at four in the morning and prepare to open the store, but would also wake up several times during the night in case somebody came for supplies. Night for him was a time interrupted by travelers he always waited on with few words yet calm kindness. At dawn he would light the burner that kept a fire going all day, and he would lean back in a fishing chair to nap at any hour; for him, sleeping was a question of moments, and throughout his adult life these had been so brief that he never managed to dream.

The house was big and had provided lodging for the Rieras's laborers until there weren't any more, because the grandfather stopped insisting on growing anything and his rickety bones kept him from riding on horseback as far as the other side of the mountain ridge to herd his cattle. Some thirty years ago her uncle had settled in there and established his business, and in all that time neither radio nor electricity ever reached him, and the filling station, so important in such a desolate area, was nothing more than a huge drum that pumped gasoline. Even while he concentrated on his business, he did not neglect the goats that, wild though they were, sometimes got help from him with pasturing or birthing. Nor did he forget to show his rifle and fire some shots now and then, so that any possible poachers or the goats themselves would know there was indeed an owner, and he was a man, and you just did not mess with the Rieras, ever since 1600.

His mare, "La Titi," for Nefertiti, because of her eyes outlined like an Egyptian queen, had thrown him recently in a sudden stop, and the uncle tried to hide his wounded pride by saying that perhaps he had gotten too fat or the mare was feeling old that day, like any woman who one day just feels tired and does not want anybody ordering her around. What at first looked like nothing more serious than a bump set off a whole string of aches and pains: prostate, ears, head buzzing and aching, weak knees, slow-moving intestines, and kidneys that, according to the uncle himself, had moved out of their original location.

Now the doctor had told him he had to rest and sleep, like any normal Christian.

"How's that?" asked the patient.

"All night and all at once, darn it!"

That was the exact advice of Don Aristóbulo Ocampo, the doctor in the area, who was older than the uncle and half deaf, half blind, and half crippled. And who, even in the silence of such solitude, could not sleep at night because he was an insomniac, smoker, addicted reader of detective novels, and half crazy. Even now in his eighty-first year, he still hoped to discover the mathematical meaning of life through books and science. He had long ago quit trying to explain his search to anybody in Olpa, because in his opinion, "Everybody here is a lower class Spanish immigrant!"

Under the pretense of coming to take care of her uncle, Berta arrived at that farm that also belonged to her and whose title and origin nobody ever talked about. The only thing the relatives ever mentioned in reference to the land was that it was no longer possible to divide it up because the family had grown too large, and above all, because it was worth almost nothing. Her presence changed Uncle Tristán Javier's life, for he had never in his many years lived under the same roof with a woman more than one degree removed from him in the family tree. She took charge of the chickens that slept inside the house, along with the rooster, the goats, and the store, Olpa's

Progress, and that way her uncle could follow the doctor's orders and begin to recuperate from his bad sleeping habits.

With Berta in charge, Uncle Tristán Javier climbed into bed, which he had not done for a long time, and got out only to take care of the most necessary functions, always in his pajamas. He happily gave orders from bed, until it was no longer necessary because his niece quickly learned about managing the farm and the goats' moods, as well as the business. She took things into her own hands and even sat in his fishing chair at the only gasoline pump in all of Olpa and its outskirts. It belonged to "Tristán Javier Riera, for all world travelers," he bragged, and it had never broken down but was always ready, under the kerosene lamp, like a front line in the region.

And one fine day, her uncle no longer had any pain, his kidneys were in their proper place, and his intestines were functioning normally. But he decided to stay in bed and rest to make up for all the time he had missed there. What's more, he decided to stay in bed for the rest of his life, and then he slept every night and every day, with a smile on his face, to make up for all the time he had not been able to dream since the day he moved to Olpa.

Berta asked him how he could sleep so much, and her uncle answered her:

"I'm behind in my dreaming."

Berta shrugged her shoulders, stoked the fire so the kettle would not get cold, and said with a half smile:

"Just like that, with all there is to be done around here."

🔟🎱 The Indian

THE INDIAN RESEMBLED Uncle Tristán Javier and the other Riera brothers. In fact, the Indian was like many Riojans: tall, dark, and beardless, with shiny, thick, coarse hair that he wore long and tied back in a ponytail. He had dark eyes, a straight nose, small ears, and very fine arms and legs that were not all that muscular in comparison with his thick waist. He did not seem to be much older than Berta, maybe ten or so years at most. Because the Indian was built the way he was, the weather in the Los Llanos plains did not bother him at all. And another reason, according to him, was that he had always been there, before all the Rieras and their goats, before the priests and police, even before the droughts, when thanks to *Pachamama*, Mother Earth, Olpa had been a land of forests of *algarroba*, white *quebracho, tintintaco, chañar* and other local trees, and the puma had been an animal not to be hunted but to be respected and worshiped. That was before the white men stripped away all those things that *Pachamama* had provided to support a jungle where the trees and animals and also her people and their spirits could live. Their elders could reach a ripe old age and teach the others what the voices of their ancestors whispered in their ears, at every fiesta or celebration of life or death. That is why they were allowed to get so old—to listen to what they heard on the inside more than on the outside. Because bodies so old tended to withdraw or separate from the soul, elders were able to serve as a medium for the voices of gods and spirits.

The Indian was sure he embodied the spirit of one of the elders that had been reincarnated in so many "sources," including ones like himself who had faced countless other Rieras in Olpa, just daring them to throw them off the land with the *algarroba* woods.

The story goes that one day in 1894 after an earthquake, an old, old Indian named Simón Fuentes showed up at the Riera place, holding up a cane tied with a white cloth like a flag, and said to Don Centurión Riera, the great-great-grandfather:

"I have returned." And he had brought with him his women and his children.

They say that Don Centurión, grieving over all the losses of family and goods in La Rioja caused by the earthquake, looked at him calmly, then turned and said to his wife, children, and workers:

"Don't bother the Indian, respect his place, but if he wants more than that piece of land with the trees, kill him without another thought and lock up the women and children so they will learn their lesson and later come to work for us."

Simón Fuentes had been so named by a Fuentes family to whom the Indian never bowed despite the punishment they gave him, nor thanked despite the training they provided (the story has it that he was educated at a seminary in Córdoba).

When that great-great-grandfather (also called "Sea Green" because of his eyes) died at the age of ninety-seven, he left a will in which he clearly stated his orders:

". . . that the Indian Simón Fuentes and his descendents not be bothered, so long as they respect the boundary of the *algarroba* forest and the women of the house and the Holy Church and any of its representatives; and that he and his family be provided with enough water to live, so long as they practice good habits that do not offend Christian morals . . . ."

So the Fuentes Indians lived there, always producing some son who could take care of that piece of wooded land only three hectares in size, situated opposite the house. The Indian and all his family would periodically go away for several months, to gather fruit or hunt in other regions or to cross the mountain range, but they always returned, just like the wild cattle.

The wishes of Tata Centurión were honored, and each generation was measured in terms of two creatures: a Riera man next to a Fuentes man, each with his own expression, his wrinkled brow, his lack of trust, his God. Each one sat in his own chair in the evening eyeing the other silently, except for the few words that had to be uttered about sharing the little water available there in the desert, according to the family law that nobody challenged. Both the Rieras and the Fuentes were losing family members, however. For the Indians, it was because of the poverty that forced their sons to work in the mines and their daughters in the cities. What caused the Rieras to dwindle in number included repression—shotgun weddings without a chance of lasting for some, forced lifelong virginity for others—deceptions, premature aging, and broken dreams from the very beginning. And now all that remained was this grim Indian in front of his cabin, a stand of old *algorrobas*, and Uncle Tristán Javier, who for months had not sat in his chair keeping watch over the Fuentes because he was in search of his own dreams. For the first time since 1894, that chair was occupied by a young woman, a beautiful daughter of Rioja, as dark as the Indian.

On the day after Berta arrived, instead of acting as if the Indian were not even there, despite the great-great-grandfather's orders that her uncle had passed on to her, she greeted him from her chair as soon as she saw him, delighted that this land was inhabited by something other than goats. The Indian, expecting the challenging look he had known every afternoon, was completely confused and thus responded to the young woman's beckoning, certain that some misfortune had occurred and that these signals were a request for help, perhaps the first those Fuentes Indians had ever received from the landowning Rieras.

Sometimes a gesture of greeting can also be a request for assistance or support, even when the person making it does not realize that is what it means. Now Berta, in calling over the Indian, rejected the traditional order of things that had reigned for over eighty years; she, a woman, traded words with him. And likewise, the Indian broke his silence, talking with her in a meaningful way. She explained to him that now she was the one taking care of the business and that she was greeting him simply because they both shared the same land and water. The Indian wasn't big on greetings or smiles, for he knew the two of them did not equally share anything; rather he was here just as his great-great-grandfather had been, a piece of grit up the butt of these Rieras.

Berta had called to him by waving her arm to get his attention because she had no flag, and that is why he walked over to her, because of the debt inherent in his ancestors' truce and because it was still 1976; he did not know yet how bad things would become. Berta got out another fishing chair and extended an invitation:

"Sit down, please."

The Indian sat in that chair, where for the first time he could get a perspective on his *algarroba* trees. They made a sound like water, like waves lapping, or like a chorus of wet creatures that made you dream of rivers, depths, and crystal-clear currents creating bubbling foam.

"It is the *Zapam Zucum*," said the Indian.

Berta had no idea what he was talking about, so she looked at him with eyes begging for an explanation. She waited while he stayed silent as he searched for words.

"It is the mother *algarroba*, whose milk keeps little children from starving when their own mothers are absent. When little children are alone in the mountains, she is the one who nourishes them with her fruits. She also punishes those who destroy the vegetation. From those who cut down the *algarroba* for a bad reason, she takes away their child and never gives him back."

The Indian had spoken slowly, looking toward the forest. All Berta saw was a grove of *algarrobas* shining as the night approached. From the same spot he saw a young woman moving among the trees, reddened by the colors of life, whose breasts were enormous and pendulous. As she moved among the branches encircled in a swirl of black hair, full of milk and life, she made the sound "*zapam, zucum,*" "*zapam, zucum,*" with each step she took. The Indian knew, just as his great-great-grandfather had known, that his purpose in living there on that land was to keep worshipping the mother who had wiped out three Riera families in an earthquake in 1894 because they had felled more than three hundred hectares of *algarrobas*, ignoring the cries of the grandmothers and the voices of the old ones. After all that death, those few Indians returned because the great-great-grandfather said: "I am returning." And they lived sheltered by the only forest of *algarrobas* that remained in the entire area of Olpa.

🔢 A Visitor

A CLEAR WINTER MORNING was dawning when Berta awoke to the sound of hands clapping in the hall and went out to find a wide and very ugly person wearing black from head to toe. A green Renault Gordini was parked at the door to the store. The visitor's face was quite frightening, split in two by a horrible wrinkle that pointed to the early loss of several of her teeth from a mouth with sagging corners. She had strange olive-toned skin, quite uncommon in La Rioja. One single eyebrow that crossed from left to right sheltered two black eyes. The dark thickness of the eyebrow suggested that most likely some strength and youth still inhabited that body that must have lived seventy years of work and watchfulness. Her bones were holding up at least two hundred and twenty pounds on a medium frame, but she projected a proud challenging look from her small head with its thin blackish hair, and she moved with the fearlessness of a cat.

Before Berta could ask what she could do for her, she had entered the house with an air of familiarity, making a lot of noise with her ostentatious way of walking. She went straight to the room the uncle had set up for himself beside the store, laughing and crying out to him in a strange language sprinkled with the dirtiest expressions you could hear in this country. And her uncle, happier than Berta had ever seen him, ordered:

"Bring a chair for Doña Lupe!"

The visitor chided him:

"You old good-for-nothing, why are you pretending to be sick?"

"Berta, bring the anise brandy!" commanded her uncle, in a state of exhilaration.

Berta brought them the brandy, and the two old people sat down at the little *mate* table and talked about everyone in the neighborhood extending at least two hundred kilometers, about problems with the Gordini, and about Machado the mechanic, who had gone off to Chile and did not return.

They talked about goats and orchards that produced nothing but annoyance, and about past times that were bad and those yet to come that might be even worse. They drained the bottle of anise brandy but remained sober; then Doña Lupe said:

"Tristán, bad days are ahead, for these *milis* aren't going to fix anything—in addition to being murderers, they are also thieves."

"No, Lupe, that can't be true; the soldiers are going to bring order and decency to Argentina, and now that we are all sick of politicians, we should give them a chance."

"There's not much anybody can tell this old lady about murderers. Lusaper Gregorian sees them coming from afar. These are crazy people, crazy in the head, you'll see, old man, these guys are all pieces of shit." Tristán Javier shook his head, so Doña Lupe insisted:

"I know, I really do know, that they killed your Bishop. What happened to Angelelli was no accident. I'm not going to tell you how I know, but it's the truth," she said firmly.

It wasn't the La Rioja brandy that made Doña Lupe tell the old man that; he had been listening to her repeat for the past forty years all the nightmares she had actually lived through in her own childhood. She did not have that face for nothing; there was a reason her smile had fallen once and for all. Tristán Javier was her friend.

"Tristán, you should consider your bishop a saint, a martyr of your church; these shit *milis* killed him. He was carrying a briefcase full of papers, with accusations, letters, petitions for the young people they are taking away, the people they are killing the way someone kills a goat. Old Man, we are living in the midst of assassins, and they have all the power, all the weapons. Nobody is safe. We have to think of something to do."

"Lupe, you're still haunted by fear, because of those terrible things that happened in your country. It doesn't happen here, and never will. This is Argentina! It was an accident, Lupe, the bishop's brakes failed or the driver fell asleep at the wheel or there was a flat tire, something like that. The military took charge to defend the church and Christian values. How could it happen the way you say? That man was the bishop of La Rioja! . . . And as for the ones they are taking away, Lupe, you know there has to be a reason. They must be up to something."

Doña Lupe refused to keep discussing it; this was not the time to drown in reasoning with somebody unwilling to see the obvious. Tristán Javier was not a bad person but neither was he one to stand up to others for the sake of uncomfortable or dangerous truths. Each person should solve his or her own problems; he was a landowner in Olpa and he believed that the state was simply protecting him.

Doña Lupe kept her source secret. A woman in labor had told her a lot more and had confessed, in the throes of her labor pains, that her husband had been involved in kidnappings and murders and that now she had nightmares because of what he had done. He was a petty officer who, on the night his son was born dead and his wife was left sterile, got drunk and went crazy, screaming before he hung himself from a tree that God was punishing him for what had happened to the Bishop.

"There's no one blinder than he who just won't see, isn't that the expression, Old Man?"

Doña Lupe was not going to waste ammunition on scarecrows, so she shut her big mouth with her best friend and stuck in her pocket some dried peach halves he kept in a glass jar. Before the winds began as usual, they said good-bye.

"You are an old fox, Lupe, don't get lost."

"A bad penny always turns up! Quit the fuck staying in bed so much, old loafer."

They squeezed each other's hands with deep affection. Doña Lupe took a few things with her from the store: alcohol, matches, cotton, disinfectant, and a round goat cheese that Berta put in a box. Her uncle had her secretly add two jars of cane honey and another bottle of the kind of brandy they drank.

"Add something sweet for my friend, for she has already suffered so much," he told Berta softly.

Before starting the Gordini, Lusaper Gregorian, chief mid-wife in La Rioja, said to the young woman:

"So you studied medicine? One day I'm going to call you to help me."

And she left, stirring up the dust, with the first shadows of late afternoon.

20 Cachirú

A YEAR PASSED and another winter arrived with droughts and extreme winds. The rainy season had again let nature spur the growth of the few trees that could survive in Olpa, and the rocky pasture that the herds of goats had been living on ever since the first governor had brought them over. That was when the Famatina mine had promised the finest gold to the hardened souls who ventured out to these vast lonely stretches. The birds of Olpa, whether from the air or their hanging nests woven of plants with sharp briars, were announcing that day and night did keep returning and that the heavenly movements were preparing both new destinies and familiar daily tasks.

From time to time Berta would get news from a traveler or from an old newspaper someone left behind; all of it echoed what the official state organizations were broadcasting: "confrontations" with guerillas who died because they were attempting massive campaigns against the forces of order; "subversives" trying to take over military barracks killed in combat with the armed forces; "seditious" elements shot down in ambulances, police stations, buildings, and bars; "rebels" cut down in factories, on bicycles, in jungles, on the plains, or in the sky.

In all the news that was getting out people were dying, and then the papers quit publishing stories of the fallen; there was no more information about any of that. It was simply not talked about because it shouldn't be mentioned, and if somebody somewhere was writing about the ones who were dying, and the ones managing to stay alive, and about all kinds of crackdowns, surely what that somebody was writing was disappearing into thin air.

Berta owned her own thoughts, ideas, and words because she kept them to herself, and even though she had access to very little information, she knew that thousands of people were being massacred and that thousands of horrible stories were being silenced in thousands of homes, spreading outward from Tucumán, where the repression had begun, toward the rest of the Republic just like an oil spill. The Triple A, operating within Peronism itself, killed or intimidated everyone who could be considered a leftist: thinkers, journalists, politicians, artists, and later anybody related to the most committed unionists in their defense of the workers. Atilio had at first refused to accept what was happening, but then an illegal army of murderers that his own party supported began to threaten him. After the coup, the Triple A grew in geometric proportion against the people as the military government took it over, the same government that supposedly had taken power in order to end the violence. Repression, constant fear, and— the worst wretchedness of all—the lack of rights were felt in every group, on every bench in every plaza, and all the white handkerchiefs that were useless except for crying into next to the statues that were also shedding tears in those stormy days. Berta realized that nobody was safe, including those who thought they were, because even the ones doing the killing and the ones out of reach of the bullets were dying in other ways. And one of these days they would be the ones shot down, when their blinders would fall and they would face their own guilt for having shrugged their shoulders at the suffering of mothers, wives, children, and anybody else whose only possession was a white scarf on which their pain was embroidered in bitter letters.

Some day, Berta thought, just maybe somebody would discover in a buried bottle the brief history of a country that was once beautiful but had not been able to maintain the gentleness of its teachers in their white uniforms, or the excellence of its universities, or even the sound of trains making their round-trip runs; a country that had managed to produce a destitute army capable of crossing the mountain range on foot under the leadership of a general with dark eyes who only wanted to free his brothers and sisters; a country where opera had been sung in the grandest and least expensive theater in the world, and at the same time, where people could let themselves get lost in *zambas* lulling the night. And despite all that, it was a country that had been unable to find the words needed to construct its history, the one that should have been written, in which all of its people were respected and cared for as the worthy and irreplaceable persons who made that beautiful country unique and alive. During those days, Argentina was like an unfinished poem somebody was keeping in a bottle, for later.

As the months passed, Berta learned to stay seated in the fishing chair, like an old person who seemed to be waiting for something, talking to herself, conversing with her people, both the dead and those still living but far away, as an owner and the lady of that farm, or wasteland, and of that business always known as "Progress." And she rode the mare with the beautiful eyes, which accepted her on her back, all through the area of Olpa and its outskirts, and people called her "Niece." Her skin became cracked and colored, she fattened up with the thick soups eaten to combat the cold, and she enjoyed saying nothing, just staying still, learning about plants that received strength from the sun and hardly needed even the night-time moisture to stay firm and full. Then she began to believe that there was somebody behind everything that nourished Olpa, and something able to keep that precious vital order of arrivals and departures in check. And she put anxiety and questioning on the back burner, choosing instead to take care of the animals, the land, and her Uncle Tristán Javier, who still had many decades of no sleep to recover from.

One night she thought she heard owls on the roof over the hall; her uncle, who still did not sleep soundly, whispered to her from his room:

"Don't be afraid, it's probably *Cachirú* moving around. Set out three jugs of beer for him on the patio and make friends with him."

He told her that *Cachirú* was the name of the owl that, according to the old people, had power over the body and soul of humans. When he perched on the eaves of a house, his screeching would inform the family members of their next misfortune, or even worse, he would sometimes punish them by plucking out their eyes.

At that moment, because Berta was not really interested in those old tales, it suddenly occurred to her to start thinking about her future, now that she had her own world, where she seemed to have been living forever. With a sigh she said to herself:

"Who knows? God will reveal it. . . . Did I say God?" That surprised her, even as she was filling the three jugs with beer that shone in the light of the moon.

20 Lusaper Gregorian

BY THIS POINT in her life Lusaper Gregorian was tired, and her legs—big as an elephant's because of swelling—barely held her up. Her body, which had seen light for the first time on the first day of the twentieth century, was set on feet already flattened by weight. But because those feet always wore formal black shoes, her rigorous and strict upbringing was obvious, despite the fact that the shoe heels twisted outwards, and had done so for at least the twenty-five years since her weight had begun to climb above two hundred pounds. In her opinion, a woman who wore slippers for anything besides housework revealed a lack of distinction. She, Doña Lupe, was quite the opposite. After all, she had been one of the very first women in the country to swear before the Rector of the University of Buenos Aires, for honor and her country, that she would fulfill the duties of a profession that she began practicing so faithfully in 1932. Her muscular arms suggested strength and hard work, and ended in small hands with short fingers, fat and cracked, dry and worn from constant exposure to antiseptics, disinfectants, and the early morning cold, as well as from boiling water.

When she was called for assistance, she would not only attend a woman in her critical moment but also cook, wash, clean the house, feed the animals, and water the plants if the patient did not have help. And when patients did have help, during the days Lusaper spent with the mothers she would teach them her cleaning methods and her recipes for spiked and caramelized cakes. This was a way of showing them that they too had power and that they should reveal it little by little to their husbands, fathers, and sons, who were used to meek and subservient women.

Lusaper Gregorian was the first Armenian in Argentina to specialize in obstetrics. In her graduation photograph, she looked quite stiff seated in the second row next to her professors; she was the best student, as well as the oldest and the most serious. She had lost her teeth, smile, and youthful freshness in the holocaust the Turks carried out against the Armenians in 1915. Those legs, now deformed, had held her up when her village was deported, and they did not stumble even when, to escape from the bayonets, she had to run like a wild animal, thirsty and crazed, through the hottest and reddest sands, stained with the blood of all her siblings, in a desert full of horrors, where mirages and the worst possible monsters had come to life. In just a few short months, practically a whole nation was exterminated; a million and a half people were murdered.

Lusaper was destined to survive, however, in that country whose over three thousand years of history of conquest and loss, subjugation and fleeting freedom, constituted more than just a place of geographic tragedy on the planet. It was a community of souls who kept trying to make something out of a legendary past that always ended in disaster at the end of each new chapter of its history. Because this was her heritage, she never lost her energy or strength of body and mind, and perhaps that is why she never considered a new set of dentures necessary. After all, she would always be a prisoner of the past, living with an urgency to get to some place that she could call her own. Not a country—that would be asking too much—but just some stretch between the sky and the earth where she could breathe without having to look death in the face while wandering to no particular place, without rights or even rest, just because she was born from a womb that at the time of birthing lacked an official place in the community of nations.

She was fifteen when she lost her parents and her siblings. She was rescued and then raised in an orphanage run by North American missionaries in the city of Konia in central Turkey. When she was seventeen they sent her to France, and from there she made it to Buenos Aires through contact with some of her surviving aunts and uncles, who had been rescued by one Ruben Effendi, a man who saved numerous Armenians hiding in the desert after the massacre. Because Arabs had also been victims of the Turks, many of them helped Armenians find their way to other countries.

Lusaper was brilliant; by the time she reached Argentina, she already spoke Arabic, French, and English, as well as Armenian. Once in Argentina, she quickly learned a Spanish sprinkled with the *porteño* jargon that she showed off with a very sensual pronunciation like Dietrich's, reciting the words to limitless tangos and *milongas* firmly lodged in her prodigious memory. She threw herself into her work at the university with aid from international donors, finishing the three-year course of study in two years and at the top of her class.

She met another Armenian who had immigrated to work for a leather company, and they married and ended up together in La Rioja, where she worked in the hospital bringing babies into the world. She also assisted births in the homes of the rich and in train cars where railway workers lived and in poor, small, rural homes, where she shared the people's beliefs and myths about *Pachamama,* and *Saramama,* the Corn Mother, and *chala,* a doll or flower arrangement made of corn husks and placed in the home as an offering to *Saramama,* the provider of fruits and grains, the source of abundance for the poorest of the poor.

After she retired from the hospital she felt freer but kept working, unable to imagine living without being involved in birthing. Her husband died at some point without anyone noticing, because he was a very solitary man who kept to himself. She had a son who was an engineer, but he did not have the patience to put up with the hassles in what he called "this crazy country;" besides, as he put it, it was enough already just being the son of Armenians. So he went to France and never came back, which seemed just fine to Lusaper because she was not afraid of distances or good-byes that, to her, were nothing more than a reason to look forward to the next meeting. And besides, there was still something of the nomad in her.

But one particular day, Doña Lupe decided it would be nice to have someone to help her in her all-night ministry with its more than a few close calls, and she came to look for Berta. With a harsh authoritarian air and her characteristic rough manner, she yelled from her still-moving car:

"Miss Niece! Let that old good-for-nothing take care of the business, and you come with me. You have to help with a birth!"

Berta heard that dry, ugly voice as if it came from the heavens. She grabbed a clean apron, put on her glasses, and pulled her hair back as if for a surgery class. Because it was during an endless siesta time, she did not wake her uncle but just left the key in the store and went out the back door that she left open. Olpa's Progress would have to take care of itself. She had the feeling that getting into that car, dressed as she was, was a little like entering some paradise that must exist somewhere or other. Because surely somewhere on this earth each person must have a place of her own, an accessible, simple paradise—not the one available only after death. Finding it was just possibly the whole point of living.

She was more sure than ever that happiness for her would involve returning to a hospital to resume her study and practice of medicine, the science of the body and all life's machinery. She was not going to be traveling in that Gordini to the university or the great health center that she had envisioned when she began her studies; she was getting into a car the likes of which could not be found anywhere except in that deserted land of La Rioja, with this woman who from Berta's perspective seemed unpleasant and who might take her against her will who knew where. But she did get in because that was the one and only path she sooner or later would have to travel, come what may.

They did not talk much during the ride; Doña Lupe merely pointed out things or cursed the rocks in the roads that she had gotten to know so well during more than forty years, and the dust that she would miss if she left Los Llanos for even a few days, and the heat that pressed in on that body already squeezed on all sides, especially in that humble yet noble car that carried her everywhere.

"We're going to make a home visit," she said to Berta. That meant they were going to attend a birth at some small farmhouse. "This is going to be a mess because she has already had several difficult labors and I get worried every time another child is on the way. And her belly is just too big."

Berta realized she was scared to death, yet also brave enough to face anything this woman might have to put up with. The midwife was repulsive, with a really gross mouth, but Berta thought that the two of them were chips off the same block.

After almost three hours in the Gordini, they reached a farm with a sign that Berta could not make out as they passed. At the door a man and six children ranging from around two to thirteen years old were lined up waiting for them, in complete silence, grubby, and full of fear for their mother inside. The man, with reddened eyes, said to them:

"She is in great pain, and has been for two days."

However, the woman in the bed smiled between her contractions and asked for the midwife's hand so she could kiss it as if Doña Lupe were a saint. Her sisters and the godmothers of her children were with her. Without letting go of the woman's hand, Doña Lupe opened the leather case, with its interior green cloth holding the photograph from 1932, and took out her stethoscope. She placed it on the patient's huge belly and without letting go of the woman's hand she put the other end to her ear. In that moment Lusaper Gregorian underwent a complete transformation: she became agile and delicate; her pupils enlarged, sending off a star-like brilliance; and it even seemed that her teeth had grown back in, while her skin turned colorful like a tuberose. With a soft maternal voice, she said to the woman as she laid her hand on her forehead:

"Alcira, let's get going! When have we not been successful?"

"Never, Doña Lupe, you've always saved me," responded the patient in the middle of a rough contraction.

"Out of here, girls!" said Lupe clapping her hands three times. "Go take care of the children and see that the man doesn't bother us! He also needs to quit fucking this woman!"

Everybody laughed. And Berta watched that huge woman change into a sprite who so delicately calmed the already worn out patient by transmitting to her the serenity she needed. The three of them in that room knew the situation was quite serious and that, all jokes aside, this was a life-and-death situation here in a spot far from any help except for what fit in the small case with the photo, and those four hands ready to assist.

The Armenian went out to talk with the husband, and he, who already had the horse ready, galloped off. Maybe she told him to leave just to get him busy at something so he could feel useful.

The woman was shaking and getting paler, and her tremendous contractions were leaving her completely exhausted. Doña Lupe firmly and calmly ordered Berta:

"Help her pant, and learn from Lusaper."

She joined three fingers of her right hand as if holding an olive and made the sign of the cross, the way Armenians cross themselves, and murmuring something in a language that sounded like cooing, she eased the woman through the complicated delivery. Afterward Berta could not remember exactly what she herself had done or even how she had helped the patient, but she understood perfectly the instructions given in a language both she and Lusaper shared, one that was neither Spanish nor Armenian. She felt great calm beside that woman who, as if in a trance, knew everything and communicated through that shining look on her face exactly what Berta needed to do without even having to ask. Berta was caught up in admiring Lusaper's skill in handling the birth, her marvelous art of obstetrics, when a tiny head appeared in the light, and Lusaper exclaimed:

"Alcira, we're almost done with this one; two more pushes and I get to go home."

The woman, by now almost completely exhausted, dedicated herself to her own dead mother and San Ramón, patron saint of births who was himself delivered by Caesarian section. From somewhere deep inside that even she had not known was there, she found the strength and managed to push.

A baby boy was born, with much rejoicing and a brief respite, but . . . the contractions began again. Once again the woman was contorted by her screams; a hemorrhage let loose and she was losing her pulse. Berta became paralyzed, not knowing what to do. Then Lusaper ordered in a clear voice:

"Raise her blood pressure; give her a shot, now!"

In a matter of seconds Berta mechanically and with all the confidence gained in her courses and the exams that she had stayed up all night studying for, located the syringe, the drug, and the vein, and restored both her own pulse and that of the woman, doing exactly as told. With that, Lusaper began to sing in her language and, smiling, yelled at the patient:

"Alcirita, get that man out of your bed. The rascal gave you two this time!"

That was that. Life went on. Two sons were born and a woman was saved. A poor man, proud of his eight children, returned from his search for nonexistent help, and the midwife accepted accolades and blessings, all the while telling dirty jokes. Night fell, turning everybody into passengers in the same boat that shone out in the darkness of that vast land, inhabited by people like Lupe, Alcira, Berta, and the father waiting at the gate, with six daughters wide-eyed at the difficulties and dangers at the edge of life, in those dry areas where everything and every person was needed and a Gordini car was as precious as a glass of water filtered by the stone that the Indian great-grandmother had left, which brought relief to subsequent generations.

The man brought out sweet wine, the women of the family served pies and empanadas, and they all grilled a young goat. It was not the time to leave but rather to stay and eat bread and give thanks for life.

Doña Lupe had put her ugly suit back on, but Berta was no longer fooled because the midwife's Armenian black eyes, deep and alive, had revealed the courage and self-confidence of a people who refused to bow down as they conquered all the deserts hate threw them into.

They drank a lot of wine, with Doña Lupe consuming more than anybody else. Close friends and relatives, neighbors, and others from all around showed up, because to that house of females had been added, both at the same time, two sons, to work side by side with the father.

When the goat bones had been stripped of their meat, and all the news, stories, and jokes had been shared, people once again mounted their horses because dawn was breaking, and the eight siblings were asleep in the house. Then Lupe, in a voice slowed by the night and drink, said to her new assistant:

"Do you know what is the only thing I miss?"

"No," answered Berta, in the same kind of voice.

"I miss the music . . . dancing the way they dance in my country."

"How is that?"

"With their eyes and hands."

And Lusaper Gregorian, the same age as the century, got up singing a strange and sweet song, and she danced, gliding incredibly softly, with the almost invisible steps of a gazelle, like cotton, or a cloud. And with her mouth shut, as if holding a flower between her lips, she hummed a happy tune with a beat like ocean waves, moving her eyes only, like a figure in a painting, as if she herself were made of paper, or of a dream. She danced like a princess, the princess she might have been in her country if the war had not destroyed it, the country that now existed only in Lupe's melody and her fingertips curving like traces of honey on a table covered with sugar.

The following day they left when the sun was high. As they drove away, Berta turned around to look at the sign at the gate that identified the property: it was called *La Renata*.

"It is a lovely name for a woman," Lusaper murmured as they passed by. "She who has been reborn."

22 Singing

ONE BIG PARTY had begun for Argentina on May 25, 1973. The Peronist government assumed power and immediately called for the release of twelve hundred political prisoners held by the preceding dictatorship. The uproar surrounding Cámpora's brief appointment as president[12] was accompanied by much activity at prison doors, where those who had fought against the last military governments were being freed. Suddenly, they changed into popular heroes whose companions and family members, along with huge numbers of ordinary citizens, were waiting for them. Those were moments never to be forgotten. As the prisoners emerged, the crowds greeted them singing: "They are leaving, they are leaving, never to return. . . . First Enacted Law: liberty for the fighters."

The demonstrators even climbed onto the tanks the army had rolled out into the streets in honor of President Cámpora; people took pictures of the tank drivers, who were all smiles because this time they were not having to fire into the demonstration. Far from it—this time the crowd was embracing them. In photographs taken of those moments, it looks as though the people have an army and the army has a people to serve. There was an end-of-war feeling, with a celebration of freedom, of triumph over silence, of a whole new era beginning for everyone, of kinship in every hug because everybody was part of a new humanity that this land deserved, forever and ever, amen.

Berta had begun her classes at the university and was pressing her first textbook against her breast, or opening it to smell the fresh paper; her mother worshiped it as if it were God the Father.

Trinidad went to look for her at her house on the morning of the twenty-sixth, and yelled to her from outside that there was still plenty of celebrating in all the streets of Argentina, and for her to come out and go to Villa Urquiza to wait for the prisoners there to be released.

"Come on, *Negra*!" She called. "Let's go, crazy girl. Today is a day that will go down in history, so come on and celebrate with the people!"

Berta felt herself being reborn during those days, though she did not know why, and Tucumán became soft and golden like oranges. The two friends had been born in 1955, the same year as the military takeover—the so-called *Libertadora*—and now they were eighteen, the perfect time to be presented with this new national opportunity that began unfolding, like a white flag on which they thought the best time of their lives would be written.

Tucumán was teeming with people at every corner as young and old alike came out to chant the phrases, songs, and even individual words locked up for almost a whole generation. Flags and posters intermingled with the colors of the season that should be called fall but that lasts only a few days in that narrow climatic region.

Doña Amalia had no interest in the celebrations because of too many bad memories piled up while she kneaded dough for empanadas. So, mixing the ingredients, with her head down and a serious tone, she called out a warning to both girls:

"Be careful!"

When the girls left, practically running through the streets toward Juan B. Justo Avenue, she just watched them. Once she was alone, she exclaimed to herself:

"My goodness, Manuel Rojas del Pino, if you were here now! You would have already hit the streets with these two . . . but remember how many times I told you? Peronism always begins well and ends badly. Out of the frying pan into the fire."

Doña Amalia was one of the few people in Matadero not succumbing to that wave of euphoria. Alone with her peeling plaster statue of San Cayetano, the blesser of bread, who held a tassel of wheat in one hand and the baby Jesus in the other, she realized that because of all the excitement of the day she had forgotten to offer parsley to the saint. She picked up a handful and placed it in the glass flower vase in front of him. Fixing her gaze firmly on that protective image, the statue standing on her kitchen shelf among the coffee cups, she implored him:

"San Cayetano, you who intercede for workers, have pity on those poor people who always end up being the victims. They believe in the people making speeches to them and they do what those people try to get them to do. Have compassion for those poor people who have nothing but their work; they are so ignorant. May my dead husband rest in peace, but they have not convinced me about Peron's *justicialismo*,[13] that bag of tricks! You, from the working class, never let me get involved!"

In the main plaza, in front of the government building, the statue of *La Libertad*[14] stretched out her strong arms toward the east. Haughty, her hands covered with blue and white ribbons and her head with doves, she certainly looked as if she had been capable of breaking her chains. Facing toward the hill tops, she was the centerpiece of the celebration, a link being created among everyone around her: workers, students, small farmers, artisans, teachers, artists, professionals, employees, owners, people from the center, from the barrios, from the small towns, young and old. There were no differences among all those caught in the embrace of the Peronist dream.

A whole country was coming back to life, along with words, gestures, people, and illusions, and they made up the chorus of cries echoing the words and feelings so long repressed: "always" or "never," "all" and "together," as well as "death" and "standing wall," and "the whore who bore you," that rhymed with all the national hymns churned out by the most recent military government. But none of that mattered now, because Berta and Trinidad were riding in one of the many cane carts going round and round the plaza, decorated with palms and flowers, as if it were Easter.

It really was a kind of Easter, for a society was being reborn and giving itself this new opportunity, erasing at least for these moments all the differences in strategy, ideas about nation and country, alliances, power sharing, and responsibility for the good and the bad. This new society was erasing the files that had accumulated to prove "disrespect," "betrayal," "insurrection," and numerous other charges those getting their freedom today had been accused and convicted of, prisoners of governments that no longer existed. In that awakening on May 26, with the pardon the day before that opened the prisons, the country had to begin all over again.

Throughout the day Berta and Trinidad danced, laughed, rejoiced at the release of the prisoners, swore, shouted, loved, and hated with all those who considered themselves "the people." They ended the night at the headquarters of the Tucumán Federation of Sugar Cane Workers, drinking sangria, beer, and dark wine with hundreds of workers and activists from the most diverse groups that at least for the moment joined together in celebration of the triumph over proscription, censure, and lack of rights. Each and every one of them cursed the military, from Uriburu to Lanusse,[15] though not General Perón, who enjoyed a special place in the hearts of almost everybody gathered there.

When dawn was making itself felt in the empty jugs of wine, somebody put a guitar in Berta's arms. She began to strum it like the Riera she was, and a man standing above her, with his eyes looking deep into hers, said to her:

"Sing something by Yupanqui."

Berta knew how to play only one *zamba* by that popular folksinger from Cerro Colorado, whom Tucumán was reclaiming as its own, and she announced it:

139

"Viene clareando."

She looked back into those brown eyes boiling with life before she started the first line, eyes that belonged to Atilio Sandoval, secretary general of the Tucumán headquarters. From that night on Atilio took her to all the places she would go with her body and her soul for the rest of her life. She set off with him, beginning in that moment of the *zamba*, toward the music that one day would be the only thing they had left, when the hurricane of that horrible period of fire and lead would be blamed on their caresses and promises.

At that moment it was the dawning of a love that smelled of coffee and a bakery when the first bread of the morning comes out. Atilio lit a cigarette to smoke and embraced the man next to him, Don Felipe Ocaña, an old railway director who had just been released from Villa Urquiza, without any family waiting for him. Their hearts had to stand together to be able to listen to such a *zamba*.

Berta sang that song of leaving, hurting, forgetting, losing a country, and being exiled on that same morning when everything was beginning; but she sang only for that man who was reconciling her to everything, including her own dead father's name.

"He's married," Trinidad whispered to her.

It made no difference, for in May of 1973 every hour was alive and both must have known that good-bye was a part of every kiss; that this was not the time to plan a future of personal projects, for who could resist the call of a generation that would not let things continue as they were?

"More than anything he is married . . . to the revolution," Trinidad clarified, with a soft smile.

Berta would never ask that man for anything, except that he stay alive.

Along General Paz Street, a short line of militants were singing: "Spilled blood will not be negotiated . . . spilled blood will not be negotiated."

23 *Yacumama*

BETWEEN THE *ALGARROBA* forest and the first pasture on the farm there is a spring, the only one left. They say that in the past there were lots of them that fed the *quebracho* trees when there were forests in Olpa, Olta, and Olma. They say that the water spoke sweetly to the gentle people who understood what plants and animals had to tell them. But when humankind went bad and sold off its wisdom of the forest in exchange for creating railway sleeper cars and other inventions, all the springs but this one retreated inside the earth because they no longer had anyone to talk with.

The spring is a lovely spot not far from the house and the goats. I go there whenever I have time, because just seeing it gives me a break from the heat. When I stop and really look at it, I always imagine a small river coming from deep within the earth. Despite being narrow and constricted, it is still forceful, which is why for thousands of years it has managed to create this oasis in the middle of the desert.

The Indian's ancestors and my own, after so much warring, had to come to an agreement so that there would be enough water for both, and they succeeded, even though it looks like there is not much. Nobody moves the circle of white stones surrounding the eye of the water, because that way *Yacumama*, the Water Mother, protects it and never allows it to dry up. There is also a cross that everyone respects because my aunt placed it there in memory of her Gringo, who went to sleep forever one day in August when both his heart and his watch stopped at five p.m. on the dot. The cross is underneath a pepper tree and bears the inscription "The hour of sacred crossing"—what Aunt Avelina says every time she thinks of him.

I like to look at the circle of stones, which reminds me of a snake biting its tail, and in that hole I see and understand that time runs like the water springing from its center. Almost two years have passed and 1977 is about to end. Miss Cholis and Coco visited us in Olpa, still in their wedding clothes. They say that in La Rioja everybody was betting that Coco was going to change his mind and leave her standing at the altar. But nothing like that happened and now they are married. Miss Cholis's former students, many of them now grown men and women, went to the church and sang them the friendship song, the one she taught the seventh graders:

"Light is fading,
the sun may be hiding,
but it is always shining—
the star in the sky
providing the friendship light."

Miss Cholis went to live in Córdoba with Coco, and they say Aunt Avelina was inconsolable during the ceremony, but that afterwards she calmed down when Cholis gave her the bouquet. My aunt had always said:

"Child, there is nothing more beautiful than being in love!"

Now, December 31, all the people—the conquered and conquerors alike—are most likely attending *Tinkunaku*,[16] that mixture of our two traditions where they will kneel three times before the child Jesus. But this time, at this *Tinkunaku*, the bishop will not be there, the one who knelt before the child to ask forgiveness for the sins of his church. He will not be there because, as everybody knows by now, they broke his neck. That righteous person came to Olpa and on his return went straight to martyrdom with his files full of habeas corpus petitions.

Habeas corpus: you have the body. That is what I see in the circle of stones on this mid-afternoon at the end of the year—you have the body. That is what Atilio advised me over and over.

"If you don't see me coming back, if they tell you they have taken me away, get the lawyers to file a writ of habeas corpus."

Someone would have to go out and repeat that beautiful phrase I have seen written on some portrait of Christ or some prophet, all blackened because it came from Cuzco. Have or get your body.

I wasn't able to get back your body, Atilio, or your brother's. I will not get to see my own mother's body aging, or adolescence flowering in my brothers.

I see you inside this white stone snake, a gift to *Yacumama*. I see you on that last day when you tried to speak from the balcony, calling the sugar cane workers, owners, professionals, students, military personnel, housewives, priests, teachers, everybody who could hear, to listen to you say that the revolution had united the people; that they were the revolution, with their strength, their union; that the revolution had already been realized when the workers created a government; and that although it did have all the flaws it was criticized for having, it was better than not having rights, because if there was an attempt to overthrow what they had achieved, especially with the blood of many young people, a time without words or ideas would come when they would be set back a distance much greater than the one they had traveled.

Atilio, your voice was cracking, you were babbling, you were broken, shirtless, desperate, but with all your might you were calling for them to support this government, which had already scheduled elections. You said that to destroy it was the worst possible road to take, and they should defend the government from the coup being prepared.

"Traitor, traitor!" they screamed at you, members of factions already opposing Isabel. In their view, no legitimacy remained and taking action was the only conceivable step. Traitor! Because you did not call for a general strike against a government that was dying.

They kept it up until you could no longer be heard, drowned out by the insults and other things they were yelling at you. Many of your colleagues left you there alone, doubly humiliated by those who were hoping for you to declare war against the government, and by the Triple A that had already sworn to get you, because you were a Peronist who was still too dangerous, unpredictable, and powerful.

And because of all that, because each one played a part in that improvised horror play, in that pathetic collective creation, you became the first one murdered in the dictatorship, even before official word of the coup had gotten out. They threw you off the balcony to silence you, before I or anybody could yell in some courtroom: "Habeas corpus! Your beautiful body, Atilio!"

But look how things are, look what the song of the water is doing; I still hear you, speaking out of this circle of white stones, from this heart that tried to silence you in La Rioja.

Dear Daughter,

I hope that you are doing well in the company of
my brother and sister, because that is how this
tormented mother's heart can find consolation.
Everything just gets worse. You have to leave,
my child, and this time I am ordering you to do
so, with tears in my eyes; get out of this shitty
country. (May God forgive me, but I am furious
even with the saints, for they are not listening
to my pleas.)

You must leave Argentina. Don't even try to
argue with me, just prepare to leave and never
return.

Mr. ThousandFive died, and we gave him a
Christian burial two days ago; he had been beaten
and tortured, even had his fingers cut off—we
don't know if it happened while he was dead or
alive—but he was just a bag of bones. We don't
know if it was the police, the army, or a street
gang; we don't know anything and nobody is going
to try to find out. All I can tell you is that I
gathered up the few pesos I had and with help from
the neighbors we were able to get him a little
spot in the cemetery and a pine coffin we all
chipped in for.

Right before he was killed, he told me to tell
you to leave, that he had overheard that they are
looking for you, looking for the money Atilio
apparently had from the headquarters, because
they think you must have hidden it somewhere.
They carried off Atilio's wife and children a
week ago and there has been no news yet. Then
last night they took your friend Trinidad. She was
nursing her baby and they took her away and told
her husband that it had nothing to do with him,
that they know he is a crazy guy and a good for
nothing—that's what they said to him—and that he
should look for another woman because the one he
had was no good. Pepito begged them to take him
because the children needed her, but they refused.
Daughter, you know that if she talks, you are
lost. She has not come back, just like the others.
Nobody shows up, nobody knows where they are;
we all just figure they are dead or in jail, but
nobody knows and nobody can do anything.

The Martínez family, the ones with the bakery,
have lost their children and they are going to
Spain because they have family there. You are
going to go there now; I have already arranged
everything with them. They are going to make
a place for you where you can help out in the
business their relatives run there. When you get
to Spain you will go look for a place called
Huelva—not Vuelva, so be sure you don't get

confused—Huelva with an "H," understand? And there you will look for a business called "Los Martínez de Huelva," which has something to do with bread.

Leave as soon as possible. You will take with you my share of the inheritance from my parents that I never claimed and that my siblings kept for me. Well, at least my pride that kept me from claiming my share has turned out to be good for something, because now you will be able to save yourself. You will go far away from here, and you will let me know how you are as soon as you can. I am staying here praying for you. You really must do as I say and leave immediately for Buenos Aires and get my money from my brother Tristán Clímaco, who has been keeping it all these years, so he informs me every now and then.

Fly away, and save yourself. Don't look back, because if you do the same thing will happen to you that happened to Lot's wife—she was turned into a pillar of salt. Listen to your mother. If I survive I will see you someday. Don't blame yourself for anything, dearest Daughter, for it is all over and done with now, and I'm sure that wherever you go and whatever you do you are going to be a good woman, a good person, and that is what counts. But please approach that Martínez family humbly, ready to show appreciation for any help they can give you. Remember that now you will

be an exile in a foreign country. You have your
mother's blessing, now and always, and please know
that I am proud of you, for all the ways you have
been so good, and that I hold nothing against you,
for you are not responsible in any way for this
miserable mess, in this city of murderers; you are
not guilty of anything. Stay pure in your speech,
thought, and actions. Tell my siblings the whole
truth and get the documents you need right away,
before it is too late for us to help you.

Your mother,
Amalia del Valle

24 Holy Wood

WHEN SHE FINISHED reading the letter that Rococo, Mr. ThousandFive's brother, had brought her several days after it had been written, she bowed her head. Sitting outside in the bad weather under the lamp by the pump, she felt once again the terror that had never totally left her, and that she kept reliving from time to time on nights filled with sleeplessness and nightmares. But this time, instead of getting upset about the incessant buzzing of horror, the real fear of something so palpable as the murder of a whole generation, her own, this time she felt the joy of thankfulness for support, for the hands that had reached out to help her, all through her life but especially during this escape. And, worn out with pain and love, she knelt on the earth underneath the stars in Olpa in the heart of La Rioja, and she kissed the hands of Rococo, who was crying from fear and emotion—his own terror, and perhaps also because this errand was the best thing he had ever done in his whole life. Rococo, the monster, the ugliest and most scorned man in all of Villa 9 de Julio, was now saving another life, in spite of himself, thanks to his gratitude to Doña Amalia del Valle and his affection for her children, who had always treated him with respect, the way their mother had taught them. He also did it out of loyalty to his brother, whose bloody body—abused in every imaginable way, broken and mutilated—he had embraced just a few days previously. He bathed, dressed, and cried over it as if it were Jesus come down from the cross. Then Rococo himself, like a grieving woman, dug the grave for the criminal who had committed no crime.

Berta, without saying a single word, took him in her arms and hugged that man who would for the rest of his life cry to the only family that had given him what he called his life, that sum of needs. Rococo and ThousandFive had faced life together, through machete action, freezing nights in Matadero, strong wine, blows, and every kind of bloody encounter that could happen in such a place. And now, this guy from whom nobody ever expected anything had taken the place of his brother to bring her a letter that could cost him his life as well as hers—the recipient and the messenger. Neither one of them at that moment was worth much at all.

Berta did not cry this time or become paralyzed. This time she suddenly felt that she had wings and could fly because the love of so many people in this insecure world had given her security. She was certain that she would stay alive and one day be able to tell this story. She was sure the day would come when she would cry at the grave of Mr. ThousandFive and hug her mother again.

And she knew that she would escape one more time, indeed, every time she had to; that she would escape in order to live and learn whatever skills she needed to survive and do it well; that she would recover from all the misery and would be wide awake; and that something would eventually happen to open up everyone else's eyes as well.

She let that man, the ugliest and saddest in the world, hug her while he cried for all the misfortune of his life, as the night gave way to a new day.

When he was able to listen to her and the letter had been destroyed in the fire, Berta told him:

"Rococo, you are a great man and I want you to know that you have saved my life."

And she made the sign of the cross with his fingers and kissed them. For Berta that cross was the point where two paths converge: the heavenly one with the earthly one.

The man smiled the smile of one who has touched heaven, and then he headed back down the road, taking with him Berta's messages to her mother and cheese from the happiest goats in La Rioja, candied grapes, figs, and homemade bread that she gave him for his return journey.

Berta woke up her uncle and explained to him that he could no longer do nothing but sleep because she had to leave right away. She explained to him that her mother had made it clear that she must go far away, with the help of the inheritance money her mother had never claimed, and that Berta's extreme need to hurry did not allow her to go into any more details.

Uncle Tristán Javier quickly dressed in his Sunday clothes and closed the business. Berta did not look back though she was grateful for everything she was leaving behind. She and her uncle went to Aunt Avelina and Uncle Tristán Nepomuceno's. They sat at the dining room table that was no longer used for anything except celebrations and good-byes. Berta began speaking, looking at her aunt:

"I am going to tell you a story, Aunt, about me and many people in this country. I don't know how it will end. The sad part, Aunt, is that all of it is true."

And the three old people listened respectfully to everything their niece told them so openly, without interrupting her, like the family they were, sharing her pain behind a closed door in that house where the door was never closed. Nobody said anything stronger than what anybody else had said, nobody blamed or reproached or offended anybody, and nobody cried. Berta was going away and they did not question it at all because they knew that what she was saying was true. And what a mother asks of her siblings has the same importance as the very word of God.

So she left La Rioja on All Saints Day, at night, in the shadows just like before, once again taking with her the blue bag, now associated with births, that still held the university notebook folded into the hem at the bottom.

She had cheated death by almost two years and she knew in her heart that Trinidad would not talk. Trinidad was probably already dead . . . Trinidad. . . . She closed her eyes, clenched her fists, felt her stomach tighten and then her chest constrict with the strongest pressure imaginable.

"Trini. . . ." she said, covering her mouth over the biggest silent cry she could offer up on that bus headed for Buenos Aires.

Al clarear, yo me iré
a mis pagos de Chasquivil,
y hasta las espuelas te irán diciendo,
vidita, no te olvidés de mí.

Zambas sí, penas no,
eso quiere mi corazón,
pero hasta la zamba se vuelve triste,
vidita, cuando se dice adiós.

At dawn I will be leaving
my land in the region of Chasquivil,
and even my spurs will be saying to you,
Darling of my life, don't forget me.

Zambas, yes, pain, no,
Is what my heart desires,
But even the *zamba* turns sad,
My Darling, when good-byes are said.

February 4, 1978

Dear Mother,
Uncle Tristán Clímaco was waiting for me when I
got to Buenos Aires, for he had received your
request. He put me up in the house where he lives
with his wife. Neither of them talked to me much
or said anything either good or bad. They were
worried about having me in their home and they
told me to go out only when absolutely necessary.
Later my uncle went with me to the Federal Police
station and talked with one of his friends; they
gave me my passport after fifteen days.

When he gave me the money from your
inheritance, he had already changed it into
Spanish pesos. He only gave me half of it, for, as
he explained, he had given the other half to his
friends so that everything would work out quickly
and safely. He has friends everywhere. He also
bought me the ticket to Madrid. When I left, his
wife told me: "Don't call us or write to us. We
don't owe anything else to your mother or to you,
so understand that you should no longer consider
us family." My uncle was always looking at me
scornfully and complaining about every room he had
to pass through and every person he had to speak

with, but he stayed with me the whole time until
I went through customs, not leaving me alone for
a moment. I have no idea what he said or how he
explained it all at every control point we had to
pass through.

When he was saying good-bye to me, he said:
"Get on out of here, and be careful in Spain for
they will be looking for you there as well. You
don't know me."

Now I am in the air and can see lightning
in the distance. They say that in Madrid it is
eight degrees below freezing and that it might
be snowing when we arrive. I don't know, Mother,
if I will mail you this letter and all the other
letters I've written to you in my heart every day
or not; maybe I'll throw this one out like so many
others. Tonight I want to tell about the last time
I talked with the midwife.

One day Lusaper and I were returning from a
delivery and she said to me:

"For Easter we Armenians paint one egg red.
The egg symbolizes the whole world: the shell
represents the sky; the outer layer of white,
air; the white, water; and the yolk, the world
of humans. The red color is for Christ's blood,
which paid for the world. I don't believe in
those things just as you don't. I don't believe
in religions, or in nations, but just look at an
egg and you will see a pure miracle, the force

of life, the mystery and grace that comes with every birth. If there is a god, he or she is in our hands when we help someone deliver a baby; if there are miracles, just look, it happens all the time. There have always been murderers but this"—she looked at her hands—"is stronger and triumphs over them."

She knew nothing about my life and I knew hardly anything about hers, but you know what, Mother? Now that I am in the air and flying away as you wanted, I am looking at my hands, my hands that have already gone through so much, and you know what? They are very similar to yours, Mother.

Berta

Viditay, ya me voy
y se me hace que no he'i volver.
Malhaya mi suerte tanto quererte,
vidita, y tenerte que perder.
Malhaya mi suerte tanto quererte,
viene clareando mi padecer.

Darling of my life, I am leaving,
And it looks as though I will not return.
Loving you so much,
My Darling, and having to lose you
Is my bad luck, loving you so much,
My suffering is becoming clear.

Words by Atahualpa Yupanqui

Notes

1. Atahualpa Yupanqui is a renowned Argentine folksinger, and "Viene clareando" is one of his best-known *zambas* (music for a traditional dance).

2. Hipólito Yrigoyen was president of Argentina from 1916–22 and 1928–30, when a military uprising led by General José Félix Uriburu deposed him.

3. General Jorge Rafael Videla became president of Argentina in 1976, after a coup deposed Isabel Martínez de Perón. He was considered a "liberal" during the 1970s. Author Donald Hodges discusses his posing as a "dove" but ends with the conclusion that ". . . the dirty war was planned from the top and . . . Videla and Viola [General Roberto Eduardo Viola] were responsible for its excesses" (194).

4. This militant group founded by Juan Perón in the 1950s did not agree with the Perón of the 1970s. Expelled from the Peronist movement, they became terrorists adept at kidnapping, especially multinational executives to finance their increasingly violent guerilla attacks against both the Juan and Isabel Perón governments. The military dictatorship that took power in 1976 quickly wiped out most of the Montoneros.

5. The "Triple A", or *Alianza Anticomunista Argentina*, was a Peronist death squad that first struck in 1973.

6. This is what the general of the *Primer Cuerpo del Ejército*, Cristino Nicolaides, maintained in his speeches, when he alluded to the fact that Argentina was a victim of an international "sinarchy" conspiracy.

7. The "*Tucumanazo*" occurred in 1969 while Roberto Avellaneda governed Tucumán Province. The suffix "-azo" in Spanish denotes "huge," usually in a derogatory connotation. Tucumán was the site of the violence. After tensions mounted between students and workers, on the one hand, and the police on the other, major violence broke out, and the Federal Police had to be called in to restore order.

8. General Antonio Bussi was the military governor of Tucumán Province, placed there by the junta in 1976. He was elected governor again in the 1990s.

9. A *peña* is a show or musical presentation, usually based on traditional or indigenous music or dance.

10. Liberation theology is a movement begun in the Catholic Church in Latin America in the late 1960s, that called for Christians to emphasize economic and social justice and equality. Among its leaders were Gustavo Gutiérrez, a Peruvian Roman Catholic priest who is credited with first using the term *teología de la liberación*. Many priests who were active in Liberation theology became victims of repression.

11. General Manuel Belgrano and General José de San Martín are national heroes because of their leadership in Argentina's revolution against Spain in the early 1800s.

12. Héctor Cámpora was elected president of Argentina in 1973 and held office for only forty-nine days. He called for new elections, which Juan Perón, in his seventeenth year living in exile in Spain, won by a landslide.

13. "*Justicialismo*" is the term Perón used for his own brand of socialism sprinkled with extreme nationalism.

14. In 1904 history was made when a woman, Lola Mora, was commissioned to sculpt a statue in the main plaza of Tucumán. She defied tradition by having her female "Liberty" face east rather than west as all the statues of male political heroes did. She was fired from her commission but completed the statue when the president at the time decreed that the statue should be installed.

15. In 1930, General José Félix Uriburu led the military coup against the popular president representing democracy, President Hipólito Yrigoyen. As a result, Yrigoyen's presidency was toppled. General Alejandro Lanusse was president during the military dictatorship of 1971–73.

16. *Tinkunaku* is a Quechua word referring to a religious ceremony blending both indigenous and Catholic traditions. At the heart of this ceremony is the Child Mayor, or young Jesus.

Historical Note

In 1930, the elected president of Argentina, Hipólito Yrigoyen, was overthrown in a coup led by General José Félix Uriburu. There followed a series of authoritarian governments through which the military either ruled directly or used force to control the result of elections. In 1943, the *Grupo de Oficiales Unidos* (Group of United Officers) seized power, and two years later, with popular support, Juan Domingo Perón, an army colonel, emerged as the country's leader. He encouraged the growth of labor unions and raised wages, and subsequently won the presidential elections in 1946 and 1951. Perón (sometimes referred to as the "Old Man" or the "Conductor") and his second wife Eva Duarte (Evita, the "Saint") were popular with the *descamisados* (the "shirtless ones") due to their focus on social welfare (*justicialismo*); however, he became increasingly autocratic as the economy deteriorated. His efforts to secularize the nation after Evita died in 1952 brought him into conflict with the Catholic Church, antagonized the devout population, and alienated the military. He was overthrown in 1955 and sent into exile.

Argentina then entered a long period of military dictatorships, interspersed with brief spells of civilian government. During that time Perón remained popular with the masses, and he and Evita became rallying points for the left wing opposition. In 1973, then-president General Alejandro Agustín Lanusse decided to allow elections that included the Peronists (and Perón himself was allowed back for a brief visit). The result was that the Peronist candidate, Héctor Cámpora, won; Perón came back permanently; Cámpora was forced to resign; new elections were held; and Perón returned to power, with his third wife, María Estela Martínez (better known as Isabel), as the vicepresident. After Peron's death in 1974, Isabel assumed control. Her regime inherited problems of inflation, constant strikes and demonstrations, and a violent guerilla campaign waged by Marxist revolutionaries called Montoneros.

On March 24, 1976, her government was toppled by a military junta led by Lieutenant General Jorge Rafael Videla, Admiral Emilio Eduardo Massera, and Brigadier Orlando Ramón Agosti. The junta systematically practiced censorship, torture, and kidnappings. The forced disappearance of people under the pretext of bringing about national peace became commonplace. Yet the officials of the military government who were responsible never admitted that these things were happening and refused up to the end to provide information on those who had been arrested by national security forces to either their families or international organizations. In many cases, people were murdered while being detained or in the hours immediately following their arrest, but the majority were imprisoned in the numerous concentration and extermination camps that the government had secretly set up. The bodies of those who were killed were buried in hidden graves or thrown into rivers or the sea, or destroyed in various ways so that the public would never know what had happened. State terrorism became institutionalized and all political or party activity was prohibited.

Such actions left physical, material, and moral wounds on the survivors and on the body of the nation itself. According to figures provided by various organizations working for human rights, there were at the least thirty thousand disappeared persons of all ages, social classes, and cultural levels, as well as a huge number of exiles in other countries and outcasts within their own country. Moreover, the military government was by all accounts a failure—politically, culturally, economically, and militarily. After suffering an embarrassing defeat in the Malvinas War (also known as the Falklands War), which it started in 1982, government turned over power to Dr. Raúl Ricardo Alfonsín, who was elected in democratic voting in December 1983—though not before the police and military had been granted immunity from prosecution for their actions since 1976. Argentina has had democratic governments ever since. Only since 2007 has the citizenry begun to see justice, as several of the people responsible for orchestrating and carrying out the crimes during the military dictatorship have been arrested, tried, and sentenced to life imprisonment.

Translator's Afterword

Viene clareando/Departing at Dawn gives readers an opportunity to remember or learn about Argentina's extremely traumatic past, reflect on its complex and ever-unfolding present, and construct meaning out of both. Through the moving personal tale of her protagonist, Gloria Lisé successfully illuminates the much larger story of a nation, indeed of entire regions of Latin America. The continuing effects of the "dirty war," 1976–83, officially named *Proceso de Reorganización Nacional* (the Process of National Reorganization), continue to be palpable throughout Argentine society, whether located within the nation's borders or beyond, through exile.

Military rule in Argentina did not suddenly appear for the first time when a general, an admiral and a brigadier general— Jorge Videla (Army), Emilio Massera (Navy), and Orlando Agosti (Air Force)—staged a coup in 1976 that toppled the government of President Isabel Perón, second wife of the legendary ruler Juan Perón. While repressive and autocratic, the previous regimes (1930–32, 1943–46, 1955–58, 1966–73), which seesawed with allegedly democratic presidencies, could not match the 1976–83 junta in brutality, repression, and the sheer number of citizens who were murdered and disappeared.

The junta was particularly effective, in part, because of support from the Catholic Church and from other like-minded military governments in neighboring countries, especially Chile under General Augusto Pinochet, Bolivia under General Hugo Bánzer, Paraguay with General Alfredo Stroessner, and Uruguay under a series of presidents controlled by the military, culminating in General Gregorio Álvarez's rule. Each of these governments employed similar tactics: raids on the homes of laborers, intellectuals, artists, and teachers; abduction, imprisonment, torture, and murder that plunged entire sections of their nations into grief, fear, and ultimately, resistance. The rationale in Argentina for the government's outlaw activities centered on the idea that the junta had to save the nation from left-wing elements, primarily the guerilla group, the Montoneros. But the junta went after anyone even suspected of being interested in or allied with the left, and ultimately sought to eliminate anyone opposed to their regime.

Viene clareando/Departing at Dawn weaves references to Peronists, Montoneros, leftist liberation theology, and a seemingly endless list of competing "isms" into the fabric of events spanning only the first two years of the *Proceso*, all as seen through the eyes of one intentionally apolitical medical student. Although she manages to escape from the government forces searching for her, news of what is happening to those far less fortunate reaches her intermittently. In the end, she is forced to flee her homeland, and becomes an exile in Spain, but she is safe.

Although the novel is not autobiographical in any way, Gloria Lisé also was a young woman when the junta came to power. As she states in her prologue, she turned fifteen on March 24, 1976, and her birthday is forever linked in her mind with the military dictatorship. At that time she was a teenager, going to school, studying music. She lived in Salta where it might have been possible to claim ignorance of the junta's abuses, but because she spent time in Tucumán with her father's family and entered law school at the Universidad Nacional de Tucumán in 1978, she understood from the beginning what was happening around her. Tucumán was considered a bastion of liberalism, of which it is said, "In Tucumán, the temperature is hot and the politics are hotter." Lisé thus heard numerous stories about the "dirty war," and eventually experienced it firsthand when people she knew well were arrested, tortured, or forced into exile, like Berta.

Tucumán had been in the government's sights even before the junta took power. Political persecution began in earnest in 1973, when José López Rega, soon to be President Juan Perón's private secretary, founded the *Alianza Anticomunista Argentina* (Triple A). The Triple A carried out a secret and illegal campaign to assassinate the opposition throughout Isabel Perón's brief presidency. Many scientists, artists and intellectuals also came under surveillance during this period, and most went into exile. Army General Antonio Domingo Bussi, one of the few military leaders named in the novel, was put in charge of the *Operativo Independencia*, and sent after former Montonero guerillas who were said to be hiding in the mountains around Tucumán. But in fact, few guerillas remained, so Bussi turned his attention elsewhere, which resulted in the disappearance of anyone even slightly suspected of opposition to the government.

Then, in 1976 Bussi and his forces supported the overthrow of Isabel Perón and the establishment of the *Proceso*, a more extensive, vicious and nationwide version of the Tucumán operation. This is not to say that Tucumán was spared the second time around. With numerous sugar refining factories and a major university, the city had a large proportion of union members and students, two inherently suspect groups. The novel illustrates the many different political ideologies that existed and the intense competition and conflict even among groups who equally opposed the dictatorship.

Berta's story of hiding and exile is one aspect of what happened in Argentina during the period of the junta. Another is the active resistance by *Las Madres de la Plaza de Mayo* (the Mothers of the Plaza de Mayo), a group of women who began gathering in the main plaza of Buenos Aires, wearing white kerchiefs, holding signs and pictures of their imprisoned or murdered daughters and sons, as well as other family members. During a period when peaceful assembly of any kind, especially in public, was prohibited and mortally dangerous, these women managed to raise an insistent and ultimately successful voice simply by their presence. Many historians believe that the fall of the military junta owes much to this daily, non-ideological, brave resistance.

Democracy returned to Argentina in 1983 with the election of Raúl Alfonsín as president, but attempts to bring the military leaders to justice were only partially successful. Alfonsín is remembered for creating the *Comisión Nacional sobre la Desaparición de Personas* (National Commission on the Disappearance of Persons), whose report *Nunca Más* was published in 1984. Led by the internationally known writer Ernesto Sábato, the commission produced over fifty thousand well-researched pages summarizing the atrocities committed by the military junta. Nevertheless, Congress in 1986, during Alfonsín's administration, passed laws to stop both the investigations and the trials of the junta's leaders. Succeeding presidents made little effort to punish the criminals because of links to the military as well as threats from them.

In the 2000s, as the Argentine media began regularly reporting on new evidence and suits against the leaders of the *Proceso*, several were brought up for trial again. General Leopoldo Fortunato Galtieri, the last president during the military dictatorship, was confined to house arrest, but he died before he could be tried and sentenced. Congress eventually repealed the laws granting immunity and several of the primary junta leaders were finally convicted: in 2008, General Videla was transferred from house arrest to prison and Bussi was sentenced to life in prison.

The trials contributed to families learning about what had happened to their loved ones. Some found grandchildren who had been abducted, or born in prison, and then when their parents were murdered, given to families with connections to the military regime to be raised as their own. Forensic evidence also provided proof of the enormity of the killings. One particularly moving moment occurred when the graves of several nuns and *Las Madres* were found. In July, 2005, thousands of Argentines, including then-senator and First Lady Cristina Fernández de Kirchner, attended a mass in honor of *Las Madres's* leaders, which was opened by some of their children. The service was a public reminder of the importance of remembering and the need to publicize the deaths and advocate for justice.

Lisé focused on memory rather than torture, and on a young woman whose ties to her family are strengthened as she succeeds in escaping the death squads, which helps to explain the reception that has greeted this novel in Argentina. For a first novel, and one written in and about interior Argentina, rather than Buenos Aires, *Viene clareando* has had great success with both the critics and the general public; it was chosen by the National Public Library to be placed in every public library of the country. Women have written to Lisé to say that, in essence, she has told their story. The response to this lyrical and forceful novel is certainly grounded in how people have lived with their memories and pain and determination for so many years. For Argentines *Viene clareando* creates connections between past and present, between public and private, and the way in which even the most apolitical citizen has been forced to confront the exigencies of political life.

The Spanish verb *"trasladar"* means to move or transfer, by crossing sides. Translating is also an act of crossing boundaries. The goal of providing access to a work of art for readers whose only obstacle is language motivates the translator, yet she knows from the beginning that a second language can never succeed in expressing exactly what had been expressed so perfectly in the original. The struggle to make *Viene clareando* available and intelligible to readers of English presented two main challenges: how to convey the pervasive atmosphere of terror produced by the "dirty war" in the lives of ordinary people; and, how to deal with the many popular culture references, both regional and national, and the plethora of regionalist vocabulary.

Both challenges were helped by my visit to Salta, Argentina, as Gloria Lisé's guest, in July 2005. The initial idea was to spend most of the time clarifying cultural references and regional expressions. What Lisé gave me far surpassed that: introductions to other authors and activists; access to historical documents, books, articles, films, newspapers, music, first-hand stories; a crash course in Argentine popular culture; visits to memorial sites; and a road trip from Salta, ever deeper into Argentina's interior, as we followed Berta's route.

The challenge concerning popular and regional culture presented itself to me even before I opened the book. The title *Viene clareando* is taken from a folkloric song made popular by the legendary Argentine singer and poet Atahualpa Yupanqui. Lisé uses his *zamba "Viene clareando"* throughout the novel.

I needed to translate not only the words but also the importance of the lyrics to the novel's goals. In his music, Yupanqui is narrator, witness and protagonist; Lisé's narrator serves the same functions. Both the novel and the music describe the pain of losing one's home, one's native land, and leaving everything behind in forced flight. Throughout the novel, words of indigenous origin or popular regionalisms not readily found in a dictionary presented me with many choices. Detailed discussion with the author herself cleared up most doubts, but many remained, proof that translation is an imperfect attempt to expand a work's reach.

Viene clareando's story is about a fictional character in a land and culture likely unfamiliar to most English readers, yet those who come to know Berta, her family, and their trials have a chance to understand the vital importance of this novel. Through it, the historical reality of the junta's regime takes on human urgency.

One is left with a sense of the overwhelming tenderness with which Lisé attempts to understand the price Argentina has paid in attempting to build democratic institutions.

Along with Gloria Lisé, I cannot thank Melissa Burchard, Leah Mathews and Karin Peterson enough for their ongoing assistance in bringing this novel into English. These colleagues in my scholarly writing group at the University of North Carolina-Asheville have read every word of the translation, several times. Not only have they given me invaluable feedback on the language and how to make it more accessible, but they also have supported my efforts at every stage of this project. The value of such enthusiastic encouragement and genuine appreciation of the worth of the novel cannot be measured. In addition, a former student, Joe Weatherall, closely read and thoughtfully commented on every chapter I sent him.

I am especially grateful for LeGrand Smith's essential role in this translation story. A mutual long-time friend of both Gloria Lisé and mine, he thoughtfully lent me his copy of the manuscript *Viene clareando* even before it was published in Argentina. Finally, my appreciation for the way the staff at the Feminist Press have worked with me cannot be overstated.

Alice Weldon
Asheville, North Carolina
April 2009